BOONE CREEK

CREEK

LAW & ORDER SERIES

By

Graysen Morgen

2017

Boone Creek © 2017 Graysen Morgen
Triplicity Publishing, LLC

ISBN-13: 978-0997740561
ISBN-10: 0997740566

Printed in the United States of America
First Edition – 2017
Cover Design: Triplicity Publishing, LLC
Interior Design: Triplicity Publishing, LLC
Editor: Megan Brady - Triplicity Publishing, LLC

Also by Graysen Morgen

Never Let Go (Never Series: book 1)

Never Quit (Never Series: book 2)

Meant to Be

Coming Home

Bridesmaid of Honor (Bridal Series: book 1)

Brides (Bridal Series: book 2)

Mommies (Bridal Series: book 3)

Crashing Waves

Cypress Lake

Falling Snow

Fast Pitch

Fate vs. Destiny

In Love, at War

Just Me

Love, Loss, Revenge

Natural Instinct

Secluded Heart

Submerged

Acknowledgements

Special thanks to my editor, Megan Brady, who isn't a huge fan of westerns, but liked this one! *Muchas gracias!*

Dedication

For my wife.

Gracias por creer siempre en mí. te quiero.

ONE

State of Texas, 1880

The 1:35 train to Tucson rolled into the El Paso Station, heading west along the Southern Pacific Railroad line, and lurched slowly to a stop. Several passengers disembarked, including a woman dressed like a frontier gunslinger in dingy, dark brown pants, squared-toed, black boots, and a light-brown vest over a tan-colored laborer's shirt. She was also wearing a tattered, brown duster and a black, flat-brimmed cattleman's hat that was so worn, it looked gray. The long blonde hair flaring over her shoulders from under the hat, and soft, hairless, facial skin, were the only things that gave away her female gender.

The ivory-white, bone grips of the Colt Peacemaker pistol, holstered in the gun belt around her waist, played peek-a-boo with the right flap of her duster as she stepped off the train and walked through the crowd. She had no belongings except the clothes on her back and a few personal items she kept in her pockets.

She ignored the passersby as she pulled the silver chain attached to the lower button of her vest, sliding the silver, round watch from the lower left pocket. The black hands were positioned at 1:40. Looking back at the ticket window on the side of the El Paso Rail Station, she noticed the schedule. The Southern Pacific R.R. train to

1

Tucson, which she'd just gotten off of, was scheduled to leave again in just over an hour. That was the quickest way to Tombstone, Arizona, the gold rush town everyone was headed to. However, the Santa Fe R.R. line headed north through New Mexico had a train leaving in ten minutes.

She walked up to the ticket window and retrieved a gold coin called a half eagle, worth $5, from her upper vest pocket, noting that she only had a few coins left. "Santa Fe Line to Albuquerque," she said, sliding the coin through the opening at the bottom.

"Train leaves from track two in eight minutes," the man replied, handing her a small, paper ticket.

She slipped the paper into the same pocket she'd retrieved the coin from on her vest, and walked away. The town of El Paso was bustling with daily life as she stepped around the front of the station. She caught her reflection in the glass window, and simply stared at the bright green eyes looking back at her. "New life," she mumbled.

On the other side of the building, she found a narrow alley running back towards the tracks. She leaned her back against the adobe wall and pushed the flap of her duster back, revealing a long skinning knife, sheathed against her thigh. She removed the knife and took off her hat, setting it on the ground next to her. Then, she gathered her long, blonde locks, tying them in a knot at the base of her neck. She held the knot away from her skin with one hand and with the skinning knife in the other, she began slicing just above the knot, until the makeshift ponytail was freed. What was left of her hair spread to the sides, touching her ears. She re-sheathed the knife and tossed the cutoff hair on the ground when she retrieved her hat. She ran her hand through her hair, surprised at how different she felt, before putting her hat back on.

The train station bell rang, announcing the next train was leaving in two minutes. She stepped out of the alley and made her way back towards the train, without giving the chopped hair another thought.

***

The Santa Fe Line passed through Albuquerque and kept heading north into Colorado Territory. The woman stayed aboard when it met up with the Topeka Line, heading east towards Dodge City, Kansas, and disembarked once more in a city called Red Rock.

The temperature was much cooler than it had been when she'd left on the first train in San Antonio, Texas, several days earlier. She pulled the brim of her hat down lower and lit a cigar as she walked out of the station. The city of Red Rock was about the size of El Paso and Albuquerque. Saloons and gambling halls lined the sidewalks just the same. She reached down, running her hand through the dirt that formed the streets, and rubbed it on her face, hoping to create the shadow of growing facial hair.

"Mister, do you know where I might find a horse?" she asked, disguising her voice low, to a man standing nearby, tying his horse reins to a post in front of a saloon.

"The livery and stable is over on Old Road."

"I was hoping to get one a little quicker and cheaper than that," she replied.

"Do I know you?" he asked, taking another look at her.

"No, and mister, you don't want to," she sighed. "I'm just looking for a horse. Simple as that." She wasn't used to bartering, not for anything.

"How much you got?"

"Two and a half eagles."

He shook his head. "That might get you a skimpy horse, but not a saddle. How far are you going?"

"What's the nearest town?" she asked, tightening her jaw. She'd had about all she could take. This new life wasn't working out the way she'd planned.

"Pinewood is about a day and half ride from here, and Boone Creek is about two days ride. It's a little bigger though."

She untied the skinning knife sheath from her thigh. "Will this cover it?"

The man took a look at the ivory handled knife and nodded. He barely had the sheath tied to his leg before the woman had mounted the brown mare and rode away.

TWO

Boone Creek, Colorado Territory 1880

The Town of Boone Creek was smaller than Red Rock, with only one saloon, doubling as a gambling hall. However, the town still had over a hundred residents living in and around the town limit, and another hundred working and living at the camp for the nearby silver mine up on Boone Mountain.

The woman rode into town on her mare, taking in the mix of wood and adobe buildings along Main Street. Thirsty and tired from riding for two days, she tied the horse up in front of the saloon.

"I've had enough of you causing trouble around here, Fred. It's time for you and your friends to go," a man yelled.

The woman turned around, watching the commotion in the street behind her. She noticed the silver badge, pinned to the yelling man's vest.

"Enough of me? Well, I've had enough of you! Me and my boys own this town! We make our own laws!" the other man shouted, pulling his pistol and firing.

With a kneejerk reaction, the woman pulled her pistol, firing two quick shots, one at the man who'd shot the lawman, and one at the second man who was sitting atop a horse with his pistol also drawn. Both men fell to the ground, bleeding from the holes in their chests. The

5

lawman lay nearby as town folk tended to him, but by the time the doctor had arrived, he was gone.

"New life," the woman murmured, shaking her head as she holstered her gun and walked into the Rustler's Den Saloon. She'd never had problems finding trouble. It seemed to follow her like a black cloud.

"What can I get for you?" the bartender asked, pulling a glass down from the shelf.

"Whiskey," she replied, placing the last of her loose coins on the bar and hoping it covered it.

"You new in town?" he asked, sliding the drink over and picking up the coins.

"Something like that," she replied. Knowing she'd just given him the last of her money, she needed a job and fast. "You hiring?" she asked.

"You don't look like a can-can dancer or saloon girl," the bar keep replied.

The woman pinned him with a stare, potentially deciding whether or not to give him a third eye whole.

A man dressed in an expensive dark suit, with a red, puff tie and wide-brimmed, black hat, sat down next to her. His thick, gray mustache touched the bottom of his jaw on both sides of his mouth.

"I don't know if he is, but I am," he said with a deep voice.

She set her whiskey glass down, having only taken one sip, and moved her eyes from the bar keep to the man.

"I'm Horace Montgomery, the mayor of this town. Welcome to Boone Creek. As I said, I happen to be in need of a Town Marshal, and since you so kindly took out the men who killed my former marshal, I'm offering you the job."

"I'm not the person you're looking for, Mayor," she replied, going back to her whiskey.

"And why is that?" he asked.

"For starters, I'm a woman, and I've never seen a law-woman in any town I've passed through."

"First time for everything," he said. "The way you took those men down without blinking an eye…hell, you could be a snake oil salesman for all I care. We could use someone with your skills around here. It's about time we cleaned up this town. Besides, you could be looking at prison for what you just did. Why not put those skills to better use?"

She finished her whiskey and pushed the glass to the other side of the bar.

"It comes with free room and board at Miss Mable's and pays $35 a month."

The last thing she wanted to do was get a law job, and becoming a town marshal was definitely not on her list, but if this was her penance for the life she'd led until now, then she would do it, and she'd do it to the best of her ability to ensure people like her never hurt anyone else.

"You have yourself a deal, Mayor Montgomery," she said, holding out her hand.

"Wonderful." He grinned. "What's your name?"

"Jessie…Jessie Henry."

He pulled the dead marshal's badge from his pocket, wiping the bit of blood on his handkerchief. "Jessie Henry, do you swear to uphold the laws of the Town of Boone Creek and keep order to the best of your ability?"

"I do," she replied, looking at the silver badge. It was a star with the words Town Marshal written in the middle, and Boone Creek, Colorado Territory, encircling the star.

"Do you promise to put the town folk of Boone Creek before yourself, protecting them to the best of your ability?"

"I do."

"I hereby declare you, Jessie Henry, the new Town Marshal of Boone Creek," he said, pinning the badge to her duster. "Here's an advance on this month's salary. You might want to..." he paused, looking at her drab, frontier-man, clothing. "Clean up a bit," he smiled. "The marshal station houses our jail. It's at the end of Main Street before the curve, across from Fray's General Trade Store. Miss Mable's is behind the saloon here in front of Six Gun Alley. The town's not very big. Main Street runs along here and turns into Main Street Curve at the end and wraps back to Center Street, which runs through the middle of town, kind of in the shape of a P. Or you can head out of town towards Pinewood Pass, just off the curve before it wraps back. Center Street will take you to the livery and stable, as well as Six Gun and Miss Mable's. My office is the large building along Main Street Curve, just before the cutoff to Pinewood Pass. Let me know if you need anything."

"What about deputies?"

"You have one. His name is Bert."

"Great," she replied, wondering what she'd gotten herself into.

***

As soon as the mayor left the saloon, Jessie removed the badge and pinned it to her vest, under the duster, and out of sight.

"Something tells me he just made a deal with the devil," the bartender mumbled, sliding another glass of whiskey her way. "It's on the house," he added.

"Maybe he did," she said, swallowing the drink in one long swallow, barely noticing the burning sensation as it made its way down to her belly. She got off the stool and turned back around. "What's your name?"

"Elmer," he said, setting down a glass he was drying with a towel, as he reached over to shake her hand.

"I'm sure you'll be seeing a lot of me."

"You'll always be welcome here, Marshal."

Jessie tipped her hat in his direction and walked out the door.

THREE

The dusty street had about a dozen residents and business patrons milling about as Jessie walked along, choosing to make her own path down the middle instead of using the sidewalk. Conversations stopped as she passed by. No one knew who she was…yet. They were simply intrigued by the newcomer. Jessie kept the brim of her hat low, more as an intimidation factor than anything else.

The clothing shop in town, called the Fashionette, was just down the street on the left side. An old, bent, brass bell rang as she pulled the door open. The inside of the small store had various upscale, women's dress suits on one side, complete with all of the attire that went with them. The other wall had various styles of men's suits with multiple vest and tie options.

"Good afternoon, sir," a man called out as he came out of a doorway leading to a back area. He was dressed in a suit, minus the jacket, with a bright blue vest and matching puff tie. He had on a white apron, covering him from mid chest to just above the knee, with a long measuring tape around his neck which hung down his chest on both sides. He was also wearing round, metal spectacles, which he kept pushing up on his nose. His thinning hair was perfectly combed to one side, and his matching mustache was so thick, it covered both of his lips. "Pardon me, ma'am," he mumbled, getting a closer look at Jessie. "I'm Ike, the owner of the Fashionette."

She'd chopped her hair off, but the baby soft skin of her cheeks, despite years of being in the sun, seemed to give her away every time, unless she covered her face in dirt, which she hadn't done that morning.

"What can I help you with?" he asked, looking at her drab attire, from head to toe.

"I need to clean up a bit," she said, using the mayor's words.

"Sure. Perhaps something more lady-like?" he suggested, turning towards the dress wall.

"Uh...no. More like that," she replied, pointing to the men's suit displayed in the window. "But less formal."

Ike pursed his lips and raised a brow. "I'm not sure I'll have anything ready right now that will fit you. Let's start with some measurements."

Jessie removed her duster, but kept her hat on.

Ike noticed the badge pinned to her vest. "Why didn't you say you were the new Town Marshal? I'll get you fixed right up," he said, stretching out his tape measure.

Jessie stood with her legs spread and arms out wide as he went to work. He started with her inseam, then her waist, followed by her arm length.

"Do you wear a corset?" he asked, not exactly sure how to measure her chest.

"Do I look like I do?" she replied, staring him straight in the eye. If her Peacemaker had been closer, she may have shot him dead.

He cleared his throat without answering, and measured across her chest. "Okay. Let me go to the back and see what I have."

Jessie stood near the wall, watching the street through the window. She couldn't remember the last time she'd had new clothes. She'd usually made do with whatever she could find.

"You're about as small as it gets," Ike said, upon returning to the front room with his arms full of clothing.

"I'm average-sized and a bit on the tall side," she retorted.

"Yes...for a lady. But in men's clothing, you're small. Here, try these pants on. This one is close in the waist, but too long in the legs, and this other pair is close in the legs, but big in the waist. The only thing I have right now is black, as that is the most popular. Also, I have a couple of white, high-collared, inset-bib shirts for you to try. The sleeves are too long, but they should work."

Jessie took the garments and stepped behind a curtain enclosed area to change. She was used to clothes that didn't fit properly. She removed her clothing down to her undergarments and pulled on the first pair of trousers. The length was okay, but the waist was a little loose. They still fit enough for her to be able to wear them. The second pair was entirely too big to bother trying. She moved onto the shirts, choosing the one that fit loosely in the chest and shoulders, but had sleeves that were too long. She buttoned the cuffs and folded them back a couple of times, before stepping out from behind the curtain, sporting her new duds.

"Very nice," Ike said with a nod. "We can fix this," he added, looking at the waist. He grabbed a set of black suspenders. "These sleeves are a mess, though. Here, try a pair of these," he suggested, handing her a set of bright red garter belts. Most card dealers and bar keeps wore

12

them to keep their long, puffy sleeves at bay while working, as well as business men who had issues with their sleeves.

"Can I have the black ones?"

"Sure," he said, handing her a different pair.

Jessie slid the garter's over her wrists and up to her upper arms. They seemed to hold the bulk of the baggy sleeves in place. Then, she put the suspenders over the front buttons on the waist band of her pants, as well as the back ones, and pulled them up over her shoulders.

"Step up here," Ike said, pointing to a small, wooden box. When Jessie obliged, he adjusted her suspenders from behind, pulling her pants up slightly, and holding them where they needed to be. As soon as he finished, he walked over to a stack of vests and began thumbing through them, obviously searching for something close to her size. "Do you have a color in mind?"

"Black," she replied, still standing on the box.

"Everything black?" he asked, looking back over his shoulder.

"Yes."

"All right, give this one a try," he replied, handing her a black, single-breasted vest with a notched collar. It had four pockets: two upper, and two lower, with five buttons down the middle. The bottom was square-off, whereas most vests had a V-shaped bottom. "I also have it with buttons that are made of tin, which would match that silver badge of yours pretty good."

"Black is fine," she said, putting on the vest.

Ike pulled the strings in the back, making the vest form around her meager bust, as he tied them tightly. It was a little big in the shoulders, but otherwise fit okay.

"I also have this one in burgundy, but I have a similar style and fit in silk, which comes in several colors…in case you want a different look, perhaps for an evening at the theatre."

"I'll keep that in mind. What about a coat?"

"Before we get to the coats, which I only have two that will come even close to fitting you, what about a tie? I have puff ties, narrow neck ties, wide neck ties, and bow ties." He pointed to the table with an array of tie styles and colors.

Jessie held them up, one by one, and chose a black, narrow neck tie. "This will do."

He showed her how to work the clasp, then helped her get it in place even with her collar and tucked under the top opening of the vest. "This here is a town coat, made of the same material as the trousers you have on. I have a few other styles," he said, handing her the coat. "But I think you'd be happier with this one. It sits just below the waist, to about where the fingers fall at your sides."

Jessie pulled on the black coat, buttoning the two tin buttons in the middle. The collar was also notched, similar to the vest she had on, and it had a deep pocket on each side.

"How about a new hat?" Ike asked, looking at the old, ratty one on her head. "I have this one here, it's a gambler-style, made of black rabbit fur."

"It looks like a low top hat with a rolled brim," she replied.

He shrugged. "Give it a try."

Jessie removed her old hat, causing her hair to fall down over her ears on the sides. It was slightly shorter in the back. She caught the odd expression on Ike's face as

14

she slid the new hat on. "I'm headed to the barber after this," she mumbled.

He simply nodded. "What do you think?"

Jessie had never been so dressed up, not counting the times her mother had made her wear a dressing skirt, complete with a bustle, corset, and six petticoats, all of which she completely hated wearing, and swore off. She felt very different.

"Take a look over here," Ike called, turning a thin mirror around.

Jessie was taken aback. She looked like a new person. *New life,* she thought.

"You're starting to look like a town marshal, now." He smiled.

Jessie Henry, Town Marshal. She shook her head, wondering if it was a dream or a nightmare.

"Well, what do you think? In my personal opinion, I think it suits you."

"Which part?"

"Well…all of it, of course. We can't have our new marshal looking like a frontier cattleman, now can we?"

"I suppose not. How much is all of this going to cost me?"

"How about we make a deal? You can borrow what you have on since it barely fits, and I'll get to work on a new suit using your custom measurements. We'll talk prices when the new suit is ready, and I know…all black," he said, holding his hand up. "For now, let's call it even at two and half eagles."

Jessie put her old boots back on, happy to have something that felt like her. Then, she reached into the pockets of her old clothing, removing all of her personal items, including the money Mayor Montgomery had given her. "Here you go," she said, handing him three gold coins worth $25.

"Your new suit will be ready in about two weeks. Where should I send notice?"

"I'll be staying at Miss Mable's, but I don't have a room number yet. I'll just check back with you."

"What about the Marshal's Office? I could send your message there."

"Sure. That'll be fine."

"Well then, good luck, Marshal..."

"Henry. Jessie Henry."

"Marshal Henry." He nodded, sticking his hand out. "Good luck to you."

FOUR

The barber shop was located at the corner of Main Street Curve, next to the General Trade store. A wooden sign hung above the door with *Fray General Trade* neatly painted across it. A woman stood inside, sweeping the street dust from the wooden floor. She wore a dark-blue, twill, walking-skirt, and a white and blue, paisley shirt with a high collar and long, puffy sleeves. Her light-brown hair was tied up in a bun, near the center of the back of her head. The few loose tendrils that hung down were tucked behind her ear.

Jessie slowed her pace, watching the woman through the panned windows and open doorway as she passed by. Pulling her eyes away from the beautiful sight, she tugged her hat brim lower, and kept walking.

"Good afternoon," a man said, finishing up with a customer as she entered the barber shop. He was dressed similar to her, but in a green vest, and without a coat. His tie was a black, string bow-tie. He wore a white apron that covered his front from about mid chest, down to his thighs. His hair was balding on top, but the few tresses he did have up there were combed over with wax to keep them place, and he had thick muttonchops that went all the way to his chin.

Jessie tipped her hat and looked around the small room. A large front window filled the space with sunlight. A single chair sat in the middle, and a table full of hair cutting and shaving tools was next to it.

"What can I do for you?" he asked, sweeping the hair trimmings out of the chair after his customer left.

"I need a haircut," she said, removing her hat.

"I see," he mumbled, nodding his head up and down at the realization she was a woman...with short hair no less, and dressed in a man's suit. "Well...have a seat and let's see what we can do."

"I'd like it shorter, trimmed neat around my ears and the back of my neck," she informed.

Most men wore their hair around collar length, or at least touching their collar, some slightly longer.

"Okay." He nodded, seemingly studying her hair before placing a drape over her to collect the clippings. "What's your name?"

"Jessie. Jessie Henry."

"Well, Jessie Henry, I'm Joe. Most people call me Muddy Joe, on account there's always a mud puddle in front of my shop when it rains." He smiled, putting some oil on his hands to lather in her hair, making it easier for his scissors to cut it. "You're new in town, aren't you?"

"Yes."

"Where are you from?" he asked, combing her hair at the crown.

"The south."

"What brought you to Boone Creek?" he continued, trimming one side, then moving to the other.

"The Santa Fe Line, and an old mare," she replied.

He looked at her with an odd expression. "You don't talk much, do you?"

"Nope," she said flatly.

"Fair enough." He shrugged, finishing the last few clippings. "What do you think?" he asked, handing her a small mirror.

Jessie was stunned. The person staring back at her looked nothing like her former self. She was still quite nervous about accepting the town marshal job, since law and order wasn't exactly a friend of hers. However, with the new town, came the new job, and subsequently, the new look. Albeit, a look she could get used to. The corner of her mouth turned up in a slight smile. She'd succeeded in her plan to start her life over, and it had been less than 24hrs. "Works for me," she said, handing him the mirror and placing her hat back on her head.

"That'll be half a trade dollar," he said.

Jessie swung the side of her coat back to reach into her upper, left vest pocket, and revealed her silver badge.

Muddy Joe nearly dropped the broom he was using to sweep up the blonde hair clippings. "You're going to have to learn to talk more, Marshal Henry. The people of this town aren't going to leave you alone once they get a look at you."

"Why is that?" she asked.

"Pretty much everyone knows we have a new marshal, but the rumor going around is you're a man from back east somewhere."

"Incorrect on both accounts," she sighed, handing him two silver quarter-dollar coins to cover her haircut.

***

Jessie noticed a young man standing outside of the Marshal's Office, when she stepped out of the barber shop. He was about her height, with a brown mustache and goatee. He had on a similar suit, with a slightly different tie and a round topped, bowler-style hat. Her reminded her of a salesman.

"You must be Bert," she said, walking towards him.

The young man nodded, tipping his hat. His brown eyes opened wider as she stepped up onto the wooden sidewalk.

"Ah, I figured you two would finally run into each other," Mayor Montgomery said, walking towards them from the other direction. "Bert, this is Jessie Henry, the new Town Marshal. Jessie, this is your Deputy Marshal, Bert Boleyn."

Jessie shook Bert's hand when he offered it.

"I wouldn't cross her if I were you. I've seen her shoot," the mayor joked. "Come on, let's go get your room set up. That's a nice suit, by the way. Ike knows his stuff," he said, walking away with Jessie.

"It's different," she replied, still getting used to the suit and the stares that came with her new position. "Does everyone in town know who I am?"

"Yep. Word spreads like wildfire around here. Boone Creek's a small town. You break wind and someone on the other end of town is going to know whether or not it smells."

Jessie nodded.

"Now, whether or not the story is the truth when it gets back to you...well...I wouldn't believe everything I've heard." They rounded Main Street Curve, heading towards the mayor's office. "This is the schoolhouse here on the left, and the church is next to it. I'm sure you'll meet Pastor Noah. He's the preacher." As they passed by the larger building, housing the mayor's office, he pointed out the livery stable and corral, which was slightly behind the marshal's building, and directly behind the supply depot and stage coach stop. "Where did you say you were from?" he asked, leading her past a residential section of town, and back towards Center Street.

"I didn't," she replied, studying her surroundings, and mentally mapping out the town. "The south," she added when the mayor glanced at her, obviously waiting for an answer.

He didn't push as he continued walking. "This is Six Gun Alley, named for all of the gun fights that have taken place here since the town was formed."

Jessie looked around. It looked like a mini town within a town, with the brothel on one side of the pathway, and the back of the saloon and bath house on the other.

"That building at the very end down there is the back of Doc Vernon's office. These small adobes along the side, just past Miss Mable's, are residential. Some have the owners living in them, but most are rented out," he informed, pulling open the door to the two story brothel. "Miss Mable, you around?" he called.

"Mayor Montgomery, I'm always available for you," she replied with a touch of mischief in her voice.

He cleared his throat and removed his hat. "This is our new Town Marshal, Jessie Henry. I was hoping you had a boarding room available, payable by the town, of course."

"Well..." she drawled, looking Jessie up and down.

Jessie quickly removed her hat out of politeness, something she wasn't used to doing. "Ma'am," she said, tipping her head.

Miss Mable looked into Jessie's bright green eyes. "I'm sure we can accommodate you. That is, if you don't mind living with a bunch of girls."

"No, ma'am. I think I'll be fine." The corner of her mouth turned up slightly. "Sixth door on the left, up the stairs," she said, then called, "Lita!"

A beautiful woman appeared from around the corner. Her olive skin, dark hair, dark eyes, and bright red lips reminded Jessie of the women she knew from her travels in Mexico.

"Lita, this is Marshal Henry. She's going to be renting room eleven. Please show her to her accommodations and assist her with anything she may need," Miss Mable said.

"My pleasure." She turned to Jessie and held her hand out. "Marshal, if you'll come with me, please."

Jessie tried not to stare at the ample bosom pushed up by the tight, purple corset, and bodice with white lace trim. Lita's ruffled skirt was cinched up on both sides, revealing the bare skin of her lower thighs and knee high, black silk stockings, which were held up by lacy black garters, similar to the satin ones Jessie wore to hold her puffy sleeves back.

"We've never had a woman here. As the town marshal, I mean," Lita uttered, grinning when she caught Jessie looking at her legs.

"You've probably never had one either…as a boarder, I mean," Jessie replied.

Lita pursed her lips and raised a brow, showing a bit of the Mexican sassiness Jessie was accustomed to. "*Quieres que te muestre? Want me to show you?* she mumbled in Spanish.

"Quizás la próxima vez. Maybe next time," Jessie replied in the same language, taking her by surprise.

"You must be well traveled, Marshal."

"Something like that," Jessie replied.

Lita moved closer and reached up, removing Jessie's hat. "Miss Mable doesn't allow hats to be worn inside," she teased, placing her hand against Jessie's chest as she handed it to her.

Jessie hadn't even realized she'd put it back on when they'd walked up the stairs. She grabbed the hat as Lita let go of it, brushing her bosom and bare arm against her when she turned to open the door to the room.

Jessie looked around at the small, sparsely decorated room. A double bed sat against one wall. A tiny nightstand was next to it with an oil lamp sitting on top of it. A chamber pot was under the bed, and a mismatched dresser with three slender drawers was on the opposite side of the room. A small washing tub sat in the corner. The square, panned window had a meager view of Six Gun Alley.

"We usually don't lock the doors around here, but since you're a boarder, you get a key," Lita said, running her hand over Jessie's as she handed her the key. "The front door doesn't lock, so you can come and go on your own. The General Trade should have anything you might need. Miss Mable has water brought in for the washing tubs and bowls on Mondays only. You'll need to leave the door unlocked if you want fresh water."

Jessie nodded.

"Is there anything else I can do for you?" Lita asked, taking in a deep breath to push her corseted breasts up higher.

"No. I should probably get back down to the mayor."

"He's probably still visiting with Miss Mable."

"Well, I have work to do. Please, don't let me keep you from…your work," Jessie said, hearing the bell ding at the front door.

Lita eyed her up and down, smirking when their eyes met. Jessie shook her head as she watched her walk out of the room. Getting involved with a harlot was the last thing she needed at the moment.

FIVE

Jessie made her way back through town, looking for Bert. The woman she'd seen earlier that day inside the General Trade store was once again sweeping the floor, but this time she was in the doorway, pushing the street dust back outside. Jessie stopped walking.

"You going to come inside, or just stare through the windows all day?" the woman asked, holding her broom still.

Jessie raised a brow and rested her hands on the front of her gun belt. "Are you talking to me?"

"Don't see anyone else stopping in the street to look through the windows," the woman said.

Jessie noted the sarcasm in her voice. She did need to pick up some essentials since she'd pretty much rode into town with nothing except her old, worn clothing. As she moved closer to the doorway, Jessie noticed the woman was alone. Proper women were almost never left alone, especially not to work a store. She removed her hat and stepped inside.

"What can I do for you, Marshal?" the woman asked, hearing footsteps on the wooden floor as she walked away from the doorway.

"How did you know it was me?" Jessie asked.

The woman turned around, dropping the broom as her eyes met the bright green ones looking back at her. The loud SMACK of the handle hitting the floor shook the fuzz from her brain. "I..." she started, slightly speechless. She couldn't take her eyes off the intriguing woman standing in front of her. She'd heard the new Town Marshal was a woman, but she'd never seen a woman in a man's suit, nor had she ever seen a woman with short hair. The skin of her face looked as soft as her own, or any other woman she'd ever met, for that matter, but there was something edgy, almost daring about her.

Jessie bent down, picking up the broom. The woman grabbed it from her hand, rushing around the counter to stow it against a shelf.

"Welcome to Fray's General Trade," she said, finally finding her voice. "Is there anything I can help you with?"

Jessie tried to ignore the soft brown eyes questioning her. "I was hoping your husband could order something for me."

"He can't," she said sternly.

"Okay..."

"I don't have a husband."

"Okay..."

"I do," she corrected. "He's...he died."

"Oh. I'm sorry. I—"

"It's fine," she replied sharply. "What would you like me to order? I don't usually do a lot of town to town trading."

"You don't like me, do you?"

"I don't know you," she said matter-of-factly. "However, I did know Marshal Milford. He was a friend."

"I'm sorry."

"Did you shoot him?" she questioned, crossing her arms.

"No!" Jessie snapped in surprise.

"Then why are you sorry?"

Jessie stared at her in bewilderment. She was very pretty, too pure to be laboring in a store. "I'm sorry Marshal Milford died."

"Mayor Montgomery said you shot the guys who murdered him."

Jessie nodded. "I did."

"Well...thank you," she murmured.

"What's your name?" Jessie asked.

"Ellie...Fray."

"Jessie Henry."

"What did you need me to order, Marshal Henry?"

"I forgot," Jessie said, getting lost in the gold flecks of her brown eyes.

Ellie broke their gaze and moved out from behind the counter.

"I do need some soap flakes, a toothbrush, a couple of cigars, a box of matches, and a jar of lamp oil," Jessie said, trying to think of the essential necessities.

Ellie collected the items, setting them on the counter one by one. "That'll be two trade dollars."

Jessie reached into her vest pocket, pulling out two silver coins, which she placed on the counter since Ellie hadn't held out her hand. She put her hat back on and gathered her purchase. No words were exchanged as she left.

***

After dropping her personal items off at her room in the brothel, Jessie headed over to the Rustler's Den Saloon using the path down Six Gun Alley that led to the back entrance. The sun had finally gone down behind the mountain, leaving Boone Creek in the dim, flickering light of the kerosene street lanterns. She was tired from her long travels, but if there was one thing she knew, trouble came out at night.

A couple dozen men were inside the saloon. Most of them were sitting or standing around the Faro and dice games being played. Everyone else was either at the bar, or sitting at regular tables. A pianist played a string of songs on the upright piano in the corner. A handful of saloon girls moved about, talking to different patrons and gamblers, encouraging them to spend more money in the establishment.

"You clean up good," Elmer said, pouring a glass of whiskey and sliding it over to Jessie.

She raised a brow and sat on the stool. The glass had barely touched her lips when a saloon girl brushed her side and leaned against the bar, holding up two fingers. "Nice to see you again…Marshal," Lita said.

Jessie watched Elmer pour two glasses of whiskey and give them to her. She pulled a handful of bit coins from a hidden pocket in her corset, and placed them on the wooden bar top. Then, she grabbed one of the glasses and clinked it against Jessie's.

"Cheers," she said with a wink and a grin before sipping from the glass.

Jessie took a swallow from her own drink, knowing it would be impolite not to drink when someone propositioned you. She watched as Lita sashayed away, taking the drinks to the men she was entertaining at a nearby table.

Elmer watched the exchange without saying anything, and quickly went back to pouring more drinks when Jessie turned back to her glass. She'd barely taken another sip when the Faro game ended and a man began yelling at the dealer about cheating. With the time it took him to draw his gun, Jessie was behind him, knocking him upside the head with the butt of her pistol and spinning it in her hand so fast, the other men barely saw what happened as the knocked out man fell to the ground.

"Anyone else have a problem?" she asked, moving her jacket to reveal her badge.

Two guys helped the man from the ground, get up and go outside.

"Who the hell are you?" one of the men questioned as he wobbled around, obviously quite drunk.

Jessie looked at his dingy clothing. He resembled a vagabond more than a gambler. "I'm the law in this town. If you don't like it, you're more than welcome to get your ass on a horse and ride off. I believe the exit is that way," she replied, pointing with her empty hand, while still aiming her cocked pistol at the men gathered around the table. The click of the hammer was heard across the silent bar as she released it and holstered the weapon.

"You'd better be careful," Elmer said as she walked back to the bar. "That was 'High Card' Jack you walloped."

"Do I look scared?" she asked.

"No...and that might be a little scarier."

Jessie shrugged.

"You made a mistake, Lady Law," the drunkard yelled, shaking his head.

Jessie moved to get off her stool and Elmer grabbed her hand.

"Give it a rest, Otis," he yelled. "He's harmless. His mouth is a lot bigger than his bite, trust me. It gets him into all kinds of trouble around here."

"Is it always this quiet?" Jessie asked sarcastically. "Mayor Montgomery wasn't kidding when he said this town needed to be cleaned up."

"Yeah...well, maybe he made a bad choice in marshals."

"No." Elmer shook his head. "I think he got it right. Just watch your back. They'll be gunning for you."

"Who?"

"The outlaws who think they run Boone Creek...starting with 'High Card' Jack."

Jessie finished her drink and waved Elmer off when he went to pour another. "I'm calling it a night," she said. "I'm boarding at Miss Mable's...if things get out of hand again," she added as she stood up. She tipped her hat in Lita's direction on her way out the door.

***

Jessie made her way around the painted ladies, waiting for callers, as she walked up the stairs to her room. Thankfully, only two had given her a second glance, and even then, they were probably only interested in the money. A woman walking into a brothel, looking for company, was something that didn't happen often. However, if you had the money, it didn't matter what sex you were.

Jessie used the dim lighting from the hall lamps to illuminate her room while she lit the kerosene lamp on the bedside table. Then, she closed the door and twisted the iron lock. After removing her hat and coat, she peeled her boots off and placed her gun belt on the floor beside them, with her pistol going next to the lamp on the table. Once she'd stripped down to her under clothes and splashed water from the washing bowl on her face, she used her new tooth brush and sat down on the bed. The lumpy, old mattress felt like a cloud as she stretched out on her back and closed her eyes. "What the hell have you gotten yourself into?" she whispered as she began to drift off to sleep.

Sometime later, the sound of heavy boot steps outside her door made Jessie snap wide awake. She sat on the bed with her pistol trained on the closed door and her eyes focused in the darkness. The little bit of kerosene she'd poured in the lamp to start it, had long burned off, causing the light to go out.

"Damn it," she mumbled, realizing a harlot had picked up company for the night as the voices of a man and a woman carried down the hallway. She got up to relieve herself in the chamber pot, and glanced out the window. The stars were still shining brightly and the street below was dark and empty. She stifled a yawn and went back to bed.

SIX

Over the next few days, Jessie began to get the lay of the land in the small town. She'd spent most of her time walking the streets, making her presence known. At night, she'd broken up a couple of fights between drunks in the saloon and theatre, but other than that, she hadn't seen much of the supposed trouble the mayor had spoken about.

"You must be the infamous Marshal Henry," a man called from an open doorway as Jessie passed by. He was wearing a black suit with a black satin ribbon as a bowtie.

She nodded, tipping her hat to him.

"I don't suppose you're interested in coming inside," he said, chewing on the corner of his brown mustache.

Jessie stopped walking and shook her head when she looked at the large cross on the roof of the small building.

"Oh, I promise you won't go up in flames. That's a myth." He smiled.

"Still...probably better if I don't take my chances," she replied.

"All right. How about I come out to you, then?" he said, walking out of the building and into the street. "I'm Pastor Noah," he added, extending his hand.

Jessie had never stepped foot inside of a church. Her mother hadn't exactly been on the church's good side back home, so it wasn't a weekly tradition as a kid, and as she got older, her lifestyle wasn't welcomed either.

Nevertheless, she met his hand with her own, surprised the touch hadn't zapped the life right out of her.

"See, I told you I was harmless." He smiled. "You've made quite an impression, and you've been here what...three days?"

"Why is that?"

"Word on the street is Jack Donovan is looking for you."

"I've been right here this whole time, so he must not be looking too hard." Jessie shrugged.

"I heard you gave him a good knocking on the head a few nights ago."

She nodded.

"That Jack," he sighed, shaking his head. "He's never going to get it together, I'm afraid."

"How long has he been a problem around here?"

"Oh, I don't know. He blows in and out of town every couple of months, but he's usually going like his hair is on fire when he's here. He's not the only one. I mean, sure, we have our fair share of unruly residents around Boone Creek. I pray for their souls to find the right path every day. However, like all towns, we have outlaws that come in running amuck. That seems to be happening more and more lately. Maybe the mayor is right."

"What did he say?"

"He stood up in front of the congregation at Sunday service yesterday and told the whole town that you were going to clean this place up, give it the law and order that it needed, and if they didn't like you or your rules, there are two roads that lead out of Boone Creek."

Jessie was taken aback.

"He has high hopes in you and your abilities."

"And you?" she asked.

"I don't know you, so I can't cast judgment. Nonetheless, I pray for you every day, just like I do for the rest of this town."

"Thanks, Pastor. I could probably use it."

"We all could. No one's perfect, Marshal Henry. Not you, not I, not any of us."

"I couldn't agree more."

He smiled. "You don't have to come inside the building, you know. You can stand right here and listen to receive the word of God. You should try it sometime. I give sermons every Sunday morning at precisely nine a.m."

"Maybe one day."

"You can still stop by from time to time, Marshal. I enjoy talking to you." He smiled again.

"Thank you."

"Be on the lookout for Jack. I don't want our next conversation to be your last rites."

"I'm not catholic."

"Well, neither am I, so that's a good thing," he replied with a grin.

Jessie shook her head and began walking again.

"He might do you a bit of good," Ellie called out as Jessie came within earshot. She'd been watching from her store front as the marshal conversed with the pastor.

"Oh, you think so?" Jessie replied. "I wasn't aware that I needed saving."

"We all need saving, Marshal."

"Maybe so," Jessie said, stepping up onto the sidewalk in front of the Marshal's Office. She leaned back against the post with her hands resting on her gun belt, and her eyes trained on the shopkeeper across the way.

Ellie went back to sweeping the dust from the inside of her store, in between waiting on customers.

"That woman hates me," Jessie muttered.

"Marshal, we have bigger problems," Bert said, hearing her mumbling as he walked up.

Jessie pinned him with a stare and pulled a cigar from the inside pocket of her coat. Before she could strike the match in her hand he blurted out, "High Card Jack is looking for you. He's down at Rustler's Den saying he's going to kill you."

"Oh, for crying out loud," she grumbled, shaking her head as she tucked the cigar away. "Let's go."

"Go?! Go, where?"

"Rustler's Den."

"What? Why?" Bert stammered.

"We can't have an outlaw threatening the life of the Town Marshal, and I take personal threats on my life seriously."

Bert swallowed the lump in his throat as they stepped off the sidewalk.

***

Ellie watched the two of them circle back around behind the Marshal's Office from her view on the sidewalk outside of her store. "I don't like the looks of this," she said to Pastor Noah as he walked past her and stepped inside to make a purchase.

"She'll be fine, don't worry," he said without looking back.

"I'm not worried," Ellie growled. "She's going to go down there and get herself killed."

"You sound worried."

Ellie huffed and walked inside. "You seem to like her."

"What's not to like? She hasn't done anything wrong, as far as I know," he replied, grabbing a can of tea leaves and a jar of quick-rub.

"You don't find it odd that she's a lady marshal?"

"People might say you're not exactly proper either, running this store all on your own as a widow, and all."

Ellie rolled her eyes. "I don't have time for knitting clubs and tea parties. I have to earn a living. I guess everyone expected me to sell the store and marry the first gentleman caller who came to my door."

"I think everyone has an opinion, but that doesn't mean everyone is right...about you, or Marshal Henry. The lord says we should all live and let live...although he uses a little more words than that." He smiled.

"That shoulder still bothering you?" she asked, ringing up his purchase at the register.

"Not so much anymore. I've been having a little trouble sleeping at night," he answered, placing a trade dollar coin and two quarter dollar coins on the counter. "Doc Vernon said to add some quick-rub to a cup of tea and give that a try."

"What? He told you to drink it?" she exclaimed.

"Sure did, and I'm going to give it a try tonight."

Ellie shook her head. "You'd better come by and see me tomorrow so I know you're still alive."

Pastor Noah laughed. "Don't worry. God isn't keeping me up at night because he intends to kill me."

"If you say so," she mumbled, smiling as she waved goodbye.

The sound of gunfire grabbed Ellie's attention. She moved to the window to see what was happening. Unfortunately, that sound was fairly common in Boone Creek, especially in the last year or so. Although mostly heard at night, there were many afternoons when the shots rang out as well.

***

"You come on out now, Lady Marshal!" 'High Card' Jack yelled from his position in the middle of Six Gun Alley.

Jessie and Bert watched him, acting like a fool in the middle of the alleyway behind the Rustler's Den Saloon, from their position atop the brothel. They'd gone through the attic and climbed up onto the roof of the two story structure from the attic window.

"This is a good rifleman position. Keep that in mind," she whispered, looking around. She pretty much had the entire alley in her view.

"What are you going to do about him?" Bert murmured, pointing down as 'High Card' Jack fired another shot into the air.

"Oh, for crying out loud!" she yelled. "At least aim at something!" she added, drawing her pistol and firing it at the ground near his feet. The bullet hit the dirt, causing dust to fly up.

"You missed me!" he shouted.

"If I'd wanted you dead, you would've been ten minutes ago. Put that damn pistol away before I knock you silly again," she hollered. "All right, Bert, I'm going to go back down," she said quietly, watching Jack move further down the alley towards the back of the bath house, which was a few buildings down from the Rustler's Den. Before he sees me, you fire another shot at his feet to catch him off guard. Just don't shoot the nitwit," she whispered, backing away from her position.

"Wait! Why do I have to shoot at him?"

"Because you'll distract him while I go out there and take him down."

"Why don't you just shoot him or something?"

"He hasn't shot anyone...yet. There's no need to shoot him. When you hear me yell your name, fire the shot," she said softly, before going through the window and into the attic.

"He's going to kill someone," Miss Mable said.

"Not if I have anything to do about it," Jessie replied. "You all need to get to the back of the house and stay down like I told you."

"Be careful, Marshal," Lita mumbled, running her hand down Jessie's arm as she walked by, following the rest of the women down the hallway.

Jessie went out the backdoor and circled around a dilapidated house, further down the alley, that was rented as shared-housing for low income residents. There were at least four of them along the other end of the alley, ranging in size. They usually housed four to eight single residents, or low income families.

Jack raised his pistol in the air, firing another shot as he moved past her position.

"Bert!" she shouted.

Jack turned towards her voice and a shot rang out. The bullet was nowhere near Jack when it hit a wooden trough, passed through and ricocheted off a tin sign.

Water began pouring into the alley from the hole in the trough. Jack was momentarily distracted by what had just occurred, giving Jessie enough time to tackle him from behind. Jack fell forward, rolling to his back as he hit the ground, still grasping his pistol. Jessie stepped on his hand, crunching down hard with her boot, while aiming her pistol at his forehead.

"I never miss," she growled through clenched teeth.

"Holy shit," Bert mumbled, stammering up to them.

"Lock up this piece of shit," she said, stepping on his hand a little harder before releasing her foot and taking his gun.

"I'll get out, don't worry," he grinned, spitting on the ground next to her feet as Bert cuffed his hands.

"You're lucky you're going to jail. Where I come from, you would've had a hole in middle of your chest big enough to see through to the other side of the street."

"Where is that?" he spat.

She leaned in close and whispered, "Hell," before shoving him towards Bert.

She stuck Jack's pistol through her gun belt to secure it as she watched Bert escort him away. Then, she walked down to Miss Mable's, removing her hat when she stepped inside.

"Good heavens, he could've killed you," Miss Mable gasped.

"If I'm that easy to get rid of, I shouldn't be the Town Marshal," Jessie replied. "Anyway, he's gone, so the street is safe."

"You really are a law lady," Lita said, eyeing her up and down from her position on the staircase.

"I'm anything but…trust me," Jessie sighed as she put her hat back on and left.

SEVEN

Bert finished locking up 'High Card' Jack Donovan on one count of carrying a gun within the town limit, which carried a simple fine; and three counts of discharging a weapon within the town limit, a much higher charge that warranted 24hrs behind bars. Jessie stood outside, leaning against a post, smoking a cigar. She kept her eyes trained on the street, all the while glancing at the General Trade from time to time.

"These are our most wanted outlaws and gangs," Bert said, handing her a pile of Wanted posters.

She stepped back inside, looking at the two, oversized jail cells, before sitting down behind her desk, which was nothing more than a rickety, wooden table with a single drawer.

"They're wanted for everything from robbing the stage to gun fighting in the street," he continued.

Jessie looked through the bundle, sighing in relief when she didn't recognize any of them. "How much has been done to shorten this stack?" she asked.

"What do you mean?"

"How many wanted outlaws have you arrested?"

"This year?" Bert questioned.

"Sure," Jessie replied, shaking her head. "This week, this month, this year...since you've been a deputy."

"We haven't arrested any this year...I'm not sure about the number since I've been a deputy. Marshal

Milford pretty much handled everything himself. If you want the truth, I think Walt was simply afraid of the outlaws. He usually let them run amuck, then cleaned up what they left behind."

Jessie's brow creased, forming a thin line along her forehead as she looked up at him. "I don't work that way," she stated plainly.

"Yeah, I kind of figured that with the way you took down 'High Card' Jack."

"How well can you shoot a pistol, Bert?" she asked, remembering how his shot had gone awry during that ordeal.

"As good as anyone, I guess."

Jessie raised a brow. "What about a shotgun?"

"Same."

"Come on," she said, standing up and tossing the pile of papers on the desk, before walking out of the building.

"Where are we going?" he asked.

She ignored his questions as they walked side by side down Main Street. "There are two things you need to be able to do if you're going to be my deputy. The first one is have presence. When you walk down the streets of this town, walk like you own them. Walk down the middle. When you walk into an establishment, make your presence known, but without doing or saying anything. Whether you can shoot a pistol out of a man's holster before his hand touches it, or not…shouldn't be the question. It should be the answer. Make them think you can by the way you present yourself…without being cocky or snide. That'll only get you killed."

The look on Bert's face made Jessie think he either wanted to take notes, or run as fast as he could.

"What's number two?"

"Don't get me killed, meaning you better know how to aim and shoot that pistol with your eyes closed," she answered as they walked into the Rustler's Den Saloon.

"Marshal Henry," Elmer said, nodding towards her. "Didn't expect to see you again so soon. I heard you had a run in with 'High Card' Jack this morning."

She simply nodded as she sat down on a stool.

"What can I do for you?" he asked.

"I'm looking for some old, empty bottles. You wouldn't happen to have any lying around, would you?"

"Oh…I probably have some in the back. How many are you needing?"

Jessie looked at the deputy sitting next to her. "I guess about as many as Bert can carry."

"Give me a minute to go look," he said, walking away.

"What are we going to do?" Bert questioned.

"Make sure we have number two covered, then we'll work on number one," she answered.

The barkeeper had barely been gone a whole minute when some drunk plopped down on a stool, yelling, "Elmer!"

"He'll be back in a minute," she said.

"Well if it isn't Lady Law," he slurred. "I heard ol' 'High Card' was looking for you this morning," he mumbled. "Looks like he hasn't found you yet."

"He's in jail, where he belongs, and where you're going to be."

"You can't do anything to me, Lady Law. I'm unarmed," he stammered. "You won't last long around here, anyway. The mayor's lost his damn mind…making a woman the town marshal. Ha!" he laughed. "When the gangs get word of you, outlaws are going to run this town." He smacked his hand on the bar and yelled, "Elmer, get your ass out here!"

"Knock it off. He'll be back in a minute."

"I ain't scared of no Lady Law," he mumbled.

"That's enough of your mouth," Jessie growled as she got off her stool and grabbed him by the back of his dingy coat and collar. The drunkard ranted and raved as she shoved him out the door and tossed him in the horse trough nearby. "Sober up and take a damn bath!" she yelled.

Bert stood back, wide-eyed. He didn't say a word as Jessie walked inside and sat back down.

"Here you go," Elmer called, coming from the back with his arms full of glass liquor and wine bottles. "Lord, Otis. What happened to you?" he questioned in bewilderment at the wet man, standing in the doorway.

"Ask her!" he spat.

"You're dripping water all over my floor. Get on outta here!" Elmer yelled, as he set the bottles down.

"I've had it with that belligerent drunk," Jessie said.

"What did you do, toss him in the trough?"

"You're damn right."

Elmer laughed. "Otis is a nuisance, but he's not dangerous. Now, his mouth is another story."

Jessie nodded in agreement. "Come on, Bert. We have work to do," she said, pointing towards the stack of bottles.

He struggled to get them all wrapped up in his arms without breaking them, as Jessie walked away empty-handed.

***

Jessie set three bottles on top of an old tree that had fallen down, and counted fifty paces as she walked backwards, looking around at the open terrain of the cattle trail. The town of Boone Creek was behind them in the distance, on the other side of the stream, settled at the base of Boone Mountain. "All right," she said, waving Bert over. "Draw your pistol and shoot the bottles."

"Right here?" he asked.

Jessie tightened her jaw and crossed her arms.

Bert swallowed the lump in his throat and drew his pistol. Taking aim, he fired three shots. One out of three hit a bottle, causing the glass to pop and shatter.

Jessie shook her head. "Do it again!"

Bert fired two shots, breaking another bottle.

Jessie nodded for him to shoot the last one with his remaining bullet, which of course missed. "Reload," she said, lining up another row of bottles.

Bert jumped in surprise as Jessie walked up behind him and drew her pistol. "I'm not going to bite you," she growled, putting her left hand on the top of his shoulder. She stood against his back with her right arm stretched out and her gun aimed at the bottles. "Look down my arm at the sight," she said. "Watch each bottle come into view." She pulled the hammer back with her thumb and squeezed the trigger when each bottle came into view between the sights as her arm slowly moved from left to right. With every shot, a bottle burst into pieces, one by one by one. She stepped back when all of the bottles had been hit. "Let your eyes be your guide. Zero in on the target, then put your sights where your eyes are."

Bert nodded before jogging over to the log to reset the bottles.

"Breathe," Jessie murmured as he took aim, first with his eyes, then moving the gun sight to that position, just as she'd showed.

BANG! The first shot he fired missed, but he never broke concentration as he hit the other two. Then, without thinking, he moved his eyes back to the first bottle and hit it.

"That's better," Jessie said, walking back to the tree. She set up a pair of bottles this time, but put them several feet apart.

Bert took his stance, focused his eyes, and aimed the pistol. His first shot hit the bottle, then the second bottle shattered with his next bullet. He looked back at Jessie who was standing just off his left side, and smiled.

"Now, you have to get faster," she informed, putting large, half-broken sections of the bottles on top of the log. Then, she stepped to where Bert was, drew her pistol, and fired consecutive shots, hitting each of the half bottles.

Bert's jaw dropped.

"Your turn," she said, putting more large pieces of glass on the log. "Find your mark, aim, and shoot, just like before, but do it faster."

Bert took a deep breath, then looked, aimed, and shot. Each piece of glass exploded. He holstered his pistol and looked at her with a shocked expression.

Jessie's mouthed formed a half smile. "Let's try something else," she mumbled, grabbing the remaining four bottles. She walked over to a large oak tree nearby. Bert watched quizzically as she placed bottles in random places in the tree and on the ground. "See if you can hit those without missing a shot."

Bert reloaded his revolver and took aim, hitting each bottle.

"You have to be faster than that," Jessie said, setting the bulky chunks of bottle in various places, high and low. "Search with your eyes, aim and squeeze at the same time."

Bert did as he was told, only missing one of the four pieces. Jessie set them up again, and this time he hit them all. He was still slower than she wanted him to be, but at least he was hitting his target. Would he win a quick draw contest, no...but in a shootout, he might do okay and at least be able to cover her back if she needed it.

"One more thing," she said. "This will help you get better and faster. Stand back behind me."

She drew her gun with her right hand and tossed a palm-sixed shard of bottle up in the air as high as she could. With a single, quick shot, the glass shattered.

"Holy hell," he gasped.

"I'll toss the glass up. See if you can hit it," she suggested, holstering her revolver.

Bert nodded and drew his gun. When she tossed the glass, he fired twice, but missed. She grabbed another piece and did it again.

"Keep trying. Focus, aim and shoot simultaneously."

After four more tries, Bert finally hit a piece, but it took two shots to do it.

"You'll get better and faster with time. It doesn't happen overnight, at least we have you aiming, shooting, and hitting your target, now."

"This is most I've ever shot a gun," he said.

"Well, no wonder you sucked at it."

Bert furrowed his brow, but he knew she was right. "What about a shotgun? We forgot to bring one."

"No, I didn't forget anything. Anyone can aim and shoot a shotgun, and hit a halfway decent target. It's a lot harder to do it with a pistol. You don't carry a shotgun in that holster, do you?"

"No," he muttered.

They both turned at the sound of horse hoofs galloping in the distance. Jessie placed her hand slowly onto the grip of her pistol, releasing it when she recognized the mayor coming towards them from town. She rested her hands on her gun belt and waited.

"I was wondering what all the commotion was out here. I thought a bunch of bandits were fighting," Mayor Montgomery yelled, slowing his horse to a trot as he came up on them. "I looked all over town for you, then figured I'd better come out myself and check things out when I couldn't find either of you," he added, dismounting his horse.

"I was giving Bert a shooting lesson. At this moment, he is officially trained to handle a firearm, at least enough to be a deputy. Before today, I would've had better luck with your horse backing me up," she said with a bit of discontent in her voice.

"You see, that's why I hired you." He grinned.

Jessie pinned him with a stare.

"Bert, do me a favor and ride Lily-Anne back to town for me," he said, handing Bert the horses reins. "The stable-hands will show you where she's kept."

"We need more deputies," she said as the brown mare trotted off.

"I'm afraid I don't have room in the budget," Mayor Montgomery said, walking beside her as they slowly headed back to town on foot.

"Have you seen the amount of Wanted posters in my office?"

He nodded. "Most of them are non-perilous, wanted for petty crime."

"And 'High Card' Jack, what would you call threatening a law officer's life and shooting a pistol around like a fool in the street?"

"Speaking of Jack Donovan, you know you can only hold him for 24 hours."

Jessie shook her head. "I know people like him. A night in jail is only going to piss him off. He'll be back for more."

"What do you suppose we do, hang him?" Mayor Montgomery scoffed.

"A better set of laws in place would be a good start. What about the more serious crimes? How often does the territory justice come by for trials? Once a month? Once a year? We have two jail cells. You want me to bring order to this town, get me some real laws to uphold. Otherwise, I'm wasting my time and risking my life for what...twenty-four hours of breathing easy?"

"Are you suggesting we have a vote to permit Frontier Law in Boone Creek?" he challenged with a stunned look on his face.

"Vote?"

"I can't just change the town laws."

"Well, you *are* the mayor," she retorted. "Aren't you?"

"Frontier Law is absolutely barbaric," he huffed.

"Maybe for some, but for others, it's a way of getting justice when there isn't any," she replied.

"And you're familiar with these...laws?" he asked, chewing his mustache in thought.

"Yes, to some degree."

"No wonder you draw first and ask questions later," he mumbled, not wanting to attract attention to them as they entered the town limit.

Jessie grinned. *No. That's where you're wrong,* she thought. "Change the laws or don't change the laws...but something has to be done, otherwise you should've just promoted Bert to Town Marshal."

"You drive a hard bargain, Jessie Henry."

"You get what you pay for in my world, Mayor Montgomery. I'm only trying to do my job."

He held out his hand. "I'll get back with you in a few days. Until then, follow protocol and let Jack Donovan out tomorrow...but watch your back."

Jessie shook his hand and tipped her hat to him, before they parted ways. The mayor walked towards his office, and Jessie headed in the direction of the Marshal's Office, just around the corner.

EIGHT

Jessie awoke mid-morning, as soon as the brothel had come to life with noise in the hallway. She'd been in Boone Creek for just over three weeks, and had developed a sleeping pattern based on the liveliness of the brothel. Most nights, it was quite noisy, so she worked late hours, walking the streets and checking on the activity in and around Six Gun Alley, leaving her to sleep later in the morning, when there was virtually no noise in the old house.

She watched the street below. Many of the town folk were happy to have her protecting their streets. Some questioned her ability, others questioned the idea of a woman being the town marshal on accounts of that behavior being improper for a lady. There were those who turned their nose up at her for dressing like a man, and there were those who praised her for standing up to the outlaws who tried to run the town. Whether people approved of her not, she didn't care. She wasn't there to make friends; she was there to do a job.

She pulled on her suspenders, followed by the garters on her arms to hold the puffy sleeves of her shirt at bay. Ike, over at the Fashionette, had delivered her new, custom-sized suit, the day before. She couldn't have been happier to be wearing clothes that fit, albeit, still a little loose.

After buttoning her vest and clasping her tie, she glanced out the window again, noticing Bert, pacing back and forth in front of the two-story bordello. She gave him an odd look and tapped on the window pane, but he didn't look up. She strapped her gun belt around her waist and secured her Colt Peacemaker revolver in the holster on her right side. Checking the window again, she saw Bert was still pacing. She shook her head and slipped her coat on. After one last check to make sure she had everything, she grabbed her hat and left the room.

"He's been out there for about an hour," Lita said, running her hand down Jessie's arm as she passed by.

Jessie spun around on the stairs, eyeing the Mexican harlot. The front of her red and black skirt was cinched up high, showing off the skin of her thighs, just above the black stockings she wore. A black, over bust corset with red lace trim, gave her torso an hourglass shape. Her dark hair was pulled up in the back with curly strands hanging down near her ears on both sides. The natural, olive skin of her face was covered by layers of make-up. Jessie opened her mouth to say something, but walked away instead, donning her hat at the front door.

"You could've come inside," she said, meeting Bert in the street. "I'm a border with a room, not a paying customer," she chided.

"I've never been inside one of those," he mumbled.

Jessie raised a brow and pinned him with a stare as she shifted her weight to one foot, resting her hands on her gun belt. "For the love of all things pleasurable, please tell me you've had sex at some point in your life, Bert."

"Wha..." He cleared his throat. "Why do you ask? And yes...of course," he huffed, sounding frustrated. "I am a married man."

"I didn't know that."

"Yes, I am... to a proper lady."

"As opposed to...what?" she questioned, ready to smack him if he spoke ill of her.

"Those women in there," he said, nodding his head towards the brothel.

"Everyone has to make a living doing something. Don't piss on someone until you've heard their story," she scolded.

Bert looked away. "The mayor is looking for you."

"He knows where to find me," she said as she began walking towards Center Street.

He fell instep next to her. "He came by the office and asked me to come get you."

"Then he's not looking for me, he sent you to get me." She checked her pocket watch. It was 10:15 a.m. "What's her name?" Jessie asked, nodding to a few town folk near the stable when they turned onto Main Street Curve.

"What? Who?" Bert questioned, looking around.

"Your wife," she groaned, shaking her head.

"Oh...Molly." He smiled.

"How did you and Molly wind up in Boone Creek?"

"We're originally from the state of Missouri. My cousin Grimsby was heading west with dreams of California. She and I tagged along, looking for a life of our own. We split with Grim in Red Rock. He went on, and we settled here after about six months in Red Rock. What about you? What brought you to Boone Creek?"

52

"This was as far as I could get on a half-dead mare," she answered honestly. Bert just stared at her. "I need to go see what the mayor wants. I'll meet you back at the office," she added, parting ways with him at the curve.

***

"Do you smoke?" Mayor Montgomery asked, offering Jessie a cigar from the box on his desk as he grabbed a match from the holder nearby, striking it on the side and lighting his smoke.

"Can't find a reason not to," she answered, taking one of the tobacco sticks. She picked a match from the holder, just as he had done.

"What do you say we get down to business, shall we?" he said.

Jessie nodded as she lit her cigar.

"I agree that our town laws are lacking. We certainly need more structure. However, I believe adopting Frontier Law is not the way to go. Wait," he said when Jessie moved to speak. "Let me finish. I received a telegram this morning from Justice Walker T. Samuelson. He's an old friend," he added, blowing out a puff of white smoke. "Anyway, he advised me to stay within the laws of the Colorado Territory for major crimes, but I can certainly up the ante if I want to for petty crimes. With that said, here's a list of changes I feel we should make." He slid a piece of paper across the desk. "I welcome your input, of course."

Jessie read over the laws. Most of them were meager punishments like simple fines and jail time. "What's different?" she asked.

"Higher fines and longer jail sentences."

"You do know most outlaws aren't sitting on bags of money, right?"

"Exactly my point. If they can't pay the fine, they'll have to do jail time. Marshal Milton was a good man, but he sat back and let people get away with too much. Over time, that gets out of hand and we find ourselves in our current predicament. The town laws aren't really changing, we're just strictly enforcing them from now on, along with harsher punishment. Hopefully, this will begin to deter some of the petty thugs we deal with on a daily basis."

"What about the more serious crimes like murder, rape, theft, manslaughter—"

"Those who commit major offenses will be transferred over to Red Rock. The territory judicial system will take it from there, more than likely sending them to the The Colorado Territorial Correction Facility up in Denver."

"This sounds like an awful lot of steps," she muttered, shaking her head.

"Jessie, we can't just go around shooting everyone who breaks the law, or hanging them just because. We don't have a judicial court here because we're a small town."

She pinned him with a stare.

"There's a system in place and we have to follow that. Now, if someone is firing a gun in public and you can't get them to stop on their own, or someone draws on you, then by all means, do what you must. But trust me, a life in the Territorial is much harder for them than getting sent to Boot Hill in a pine box."

"How many outlaws have been sent to Territorial from here?"

"None," he replied. "That's why I hired you. The bandits who think they run this town have a choice to make the next time they come here running amuck."

"Territorial or Boot Hill?"

"Correct." He smiled.

"What about more deputies?" she asked.

He shook his head. "It's just not in the budget, right now."

Jessie tightened her jaw and folded the paper, shoving it inside her inner coat pocket. "I'll get the new law signs hung up before the sun sets," she said, standing to leave.

***

A few nights later, Jessie sat at a table in the back corner at the Rustler's Den, sipping a cup of coffee, anticipating a long night, while she watched the patrons dancing, drinking, gambling, and otherwise having a good time. Most of the town folk hadn't had much to say about the new law signs. As long as they didn't carry a gun within the town limit, or do anything stupid, the new punishments didn't affect them.

"You're going to piss a lot of people off," Lita said, sitting on the edge of the table with her leg up against Jessie's, giving her a nice view of the ample bosom pushing up out of the top of her corset, and bare skin of her upper thigh.

"How so?" Jessie asked, taking a long look at the offering.

"Threatening these men with the Territorial or Boot Hill isn't a good idea."

"It's not really a threat, and I didn't make it. These laws have been here since the town was established. They're just now being enforced."

"Order a drink," Lita said.

"What? Why?"

"Otherwise, it looks like I'm sitting here conversing instead of selling."

"Oh, you're trying, but it's not working." Jessie's mouth turned up in a half grin.

Lita raised a brow. "Maybe I should try harder."

Jessie shook her head. "I'm afraid my night is full." She winked and tipped her hat as she stood up.

Lita grabbed her arm. "There's always next time."

"You seem to have an admirer," Jessie said, noticing the piano player on the other side of the room hadn't taken his eyes off Lita since she sat down.

"You mean, Clayton?" Lita laughed. "He wants to ride off into the sunset together."

"What's wrong with that? Isn't it what most women want?"

"Do I look like most women?" Lita raised a brow.

Jessie shook her head. "I guess I don't either," she replied, pulling free from her grasp.

"*No puedes decir que no para siempre.* You can't say no forever," she said.

"*Nunca he dicho que no.* I never said no," Jessie countered, walking away.

NINE

It had been over two weeks since the signs were posted, and so far, the town folk were adhering to the laws and leaving their guns at home. Jessie had still spent most nights breaking up fights between miners and ranchers at the gambling tables, promising to ban them from the town if they didn't knock it off.

"It's finally quiet out here," Bert said, walking beside her as they turned off Six Gun Alley onto Center Street, taking their usual evening stroll through town.

"It's still early yet," she replied, checking her watch.

"Pearl Hall is busy," he muttered. "Must be the new show."

"Let's check it out," she said, heading in that direction.

The large theatre was bustling with people when they entered. There were five wall to wall rows down front by the stage, several tables in the back behind them, and balcony boxes on both sides. Every available seat was taken, leaving standing room only by the door.

Jessie waved off a dancing girl, headed towards her, serving drinks. She leaned against the back wall, resting her hands on her gun belt, as the next act in the show began. Tobias Freemont, the theatre manager, stepped out from behind the curtain. "Please welcome the Bennett Sisters, a traveling act from San Francisco," he said.

Boone Creek

The pianist began a soft melody on the upright that sat beside the stage platform. The handful of violinists next to him joined in as Tobias opened the curtain. Three women appeared as the drapery began to split, all with dark-brown hair, braided and twisted up in a bun with a feather sticking out on the side. They wore low-cut, off the shoulder dresses with small bustles. Each of them wore a different color, one in blue, one in yellow, and the other in pink. Their hair feathers matched their dresses, as did the paper fans they waved near their faces.

The men in the rows down front hooted and hollered as the women smiled, winked, and blew kisses. When the song tempo rose to a more upbeat, saloon-style tune, the women began a choreographed dance. They twirled around the stage, holding their skirts, and kicking their legs out in an exciting performance. The audience cheered and clapped in time with the music. It wasn't long before the rowdy men in the front began to get out of hand. Two of them reached onto the stage, trying to grab the women, while another pulled a pair of pistols from his waist belt, firing them each twice in the air. Spectators began to disperse in all directions.

"Damn it," Jessie growled. "Come on," she said, leading Bert through the scattering crowd.

"This one's mine, boys! You can have the other two!" the man with the guns yelled to his two followers who had been trying to grab the women. He held the woman in blue tightly against him.

"Hand over the pistols and let her go!" Jessie yelled, finally making her way down front. "Bert, take the flank!"

"Oh, come on, now. We're only trying to have a little fun," he said.

58

"Give me your guns!" Jessie growled.

The man had the woman in his left arm, still holding a pistol in his left hand. With the second pistol in his right hand, he began to move his arm.

"Don't you draw on me, it'll be the last thing you ever do," she sneered, holding her hand on the ivory grip of her pistol. "Give 'em here, now!"

Neither Jessie nor Bert saw the other two men scurry off with the last of the crowd as Jessie flashed her badge.

"You're under arrest for carrying a gun within the town limit and discharging a gun within the town limit."

"You can't arrest me," he laughed. "I'm not scared of no law lady."

"I'm not going to ask again. Give me your guns," Jessie yelled.

The woman in his arms stomped on his foot, causing him to jerk around. She ran as fast as she could once she was able to wiggle free. The man spun in her direction, firing the gun three times. The dancing woman had already gone behind the curtain, out of sight, but the theatre manager had been close by, trying to help her escape. He was hit in the upper right chest by one of the bullets, and quickly fell to the floor.

The shooter glanced down at the bleeding man as Jessie pounced, knocking him to ground. Both of the guns he was holding went off during the struggle, ricocheting bullets off the walls as Bert and Jessie wrangled him into the handcuffs and kicked the pistols away.

"Holy shit," Bert mumbled, holding the outlaw still while Jessie ran over, trying to stop the blood leaking out of the hole near the theatre manager's shoulder.

"Hold on, Tobias. Doc Vernon is on the way," she said, hoping someone had summoned the town doctor. She took her coat off and held it over the hole, pushing down as hard as she could to keep pressure on the wound. "Get that piece of shit out of here," she said to Bert.

***

By the time Doc Vernon had arrived from the other end of town, Tobias had nearly bled out. He cut the wound open right there on the stage floor, trying to stop the bleeding, but it was too late. Tobias was pronounced dead ten minutes later, some twenty minutes after being shot.

"You did all you could," Doc Vernon said, wiping the blood from his hands before placing one on Jessie's shoulder. The sleeves of her white shirt were bright red with blood, as were her hands. He handed her a clean rag.

Mayor Montgomery arrived with Pastor Noah not long after.

"Who did this?" the mayor asked.

Jessie shook her head. "I think I heard the other two guys call him Shamus or something like that, before they ran off. He's over in the jail, so I'll find out in a bit."

"Shamus...Shamus Maguire?"

"You know him?"

"He's the leader of the Dirty Boys Gang. He usually comes through here about once a year, laying claim to whatever he thinks is his. He robbed the hotel the last time he was here. Thankfully, he didn't get much because it had all been transferred to the bank that morning."

"Why wasn't he prosecuted?"

"Walt Milton couldn't catch him...or wouldn't try. Who knows." He shrugged.

"He's going to hang for this. I'll see to it myself if the justice disagrees," she said in a low tone as she picked her hat up off the ground.

After giving Tobias's body last rites, Pastor Noah walked over to them.

"I thought you weren't Catholic?" Jessie said.

"I'm not, but Tobias was. He still came to my church every Sunday anyway. What about you, Marshal? Any religious beliefs I should know about?"

"Nope," she said flatly, sliding her hat onto her head. She grabbed her bloody jacket from the floor as Tobias's body was carried away. She removed the couple of things from her pockets, and tossed it in a trash barrel. "Gentlemen, if you'll excuse me, I have work to do."

Both men watched her walk all the way to the exit.

"I pray for her," Pastor Noah said. "Every night."

"Because she's a not a proper woman?" the mayor asked.

"No." Pastor Noah shook his head. "Because there's something deep down inside of her that makes her do what she does. Something I don't think any of us could ever understand."

"What makes you say that?"

"Call it preacher's intuition." He smiled thinly.

"Maybe she had a bad childhood," the mayor said. "All I care about is her bringing law and order back to this town. And so far, she's doing a hell of a good job. Pardon my language, Pastor."

"Oh, no pardon needed. Hell is but a word, unlike any other, in my book."

"Do you disagree with me making her town marshal?"

"Quite the contrary, actually," Pastor Noah replied. "I think she's good for this town."

***

Jessie had put her arms in a trough outside of the theatre, wetting her shirt sleeves from the elbow down to rinse out some of the blood. The tinged sleeves of her shirt, along with her gun and badge being in plain sight from not wearing her jacket, made her look quite menacing.

"Ohhh, Lady Law got herself into a mess now," Otis uttered as he stumbled around near the stage office, across the street from the theatre.

"Give it a rest you old bag, before I dunk you again," she sneered.

"I could have charges brought on you for that!" he yelled.

Jessie spun around with her hand on her pistol. "Give me a reason...I've had a bad night, so it'll only take one," she said through gritted teeth as her fingers tapped the ivory grips.

"Hey, I don't want any trouble," he stammered holding his hands up.

"Go dry out somewhere," she snapped, turning and heading towards the Marshal's Office, which was somewhat adjacent to the theatre, and on the corner where Main Street turned into Main Street Curve.

All was quiet at the General Trade as Jessie walked past. She glanced up at the window to the second floor, pausing briefly when the curtain shifted.

***

"Shamus Maguire, you're hereby charged with carrying a gun within the town limit; discharging a gun within the town limit; attempted kidnapping; and murder," Jessie said, standing outside of the locked cell with her arms crossed. "Because of these charges, you'll be held here until a trial date is set for you to go in front of the territory justice."

The red-haired man on the side of the bars had scruffy facial hair with a thin mustache. He was wearing worn, frontier clothing, similar to what Jessie had been wearing when she'd first arrived in town.

"You can't do anything to me," he laughed, spitting on the ground near her boots.

"I should've shot you when I had the chance," she muttered, shaking her head. "I'll certainly be present to watch your feet dangle when they hang you."

"That'll never happen. I'll be out of here in no time. You wait and see...law lady," he sneered with a grin.

Jessie clenched her jaw and stepped away before she drew her gun and put him out of his own misery like a downed horse.

***

"Oh, good heavens!" Miss Mable gasped, seeing the blood-tinged sleeves of Jessie's shirt when she walked inside the brothel.

"*Dios mío,*" Lita whispered with her hands over her mouth. "Are you okay?" she asked, rushing to her.

"I'm fine. It's...it's not mine," Jessie mumbled, removing her hat. Lita looped her arm through Jessie's and remained against her side.

"Tobias?" Miss Mable said.

Jessie nodded.

"No," Miss Mable cried. "He was a sweet man." She wiped her watery eyes with a handkerchief and sat down in a nearby chair. "Did you know him?"

"Unfortunately, tonight was my first time at Pearl Hall, other than to introduce myself when I first arrived. I'd only spoken to him that one time, but he seemed genuine."

"Oh, that he was, for sure."

"If you'll excuse me, I think I'm going to call it a night." Jessie smiled thinly and turned towards the staircase, with Lita still attached to her.

"Marshal," Miss Mable called when she was halfway up. "The mayor couldn't have picked a better person to bring law and order back to this town. I, as I'm sure the rest of the town feels the same way, am thankful you came to Boone Creek."

Jessie nodded and continued up. "I don't need assistance," she said to Lita, when she reached her door.

"I know. I wanted..." Lita paused.

Before Jessie knew what was happening, Lita's lips were on hers. It had been quite a while since she'd felt the sensation of another woman's affections. Her body began to relax against Lita's as the kiss deepened. Lita grabbed Jessie's hand, placing it on her corset-covered breast.

Jessie knew she could have this woman...all night, every night, if that was what she wanted, but it wasn't what she wanted, at least not right now. Jessie broke the kiss and pulled away.

"Perhaps another time," Lita murmured, kissing her cheek.

"Maybe," Jessie said, before going into her room and closing the door.

TEN

The next day, Jessie sat in Mayor Montgomery's office, staring out the window as he spoke.

"You did everything you could last night, Jessie. No one could've saved Tobias, not even Doc Vernon," he sighed. "It was a careless, unjustified action."

"It was murder," she said, pulling her eyes to his. "Shamus Maguire knew exactly what he was doing, he just hit the wrong person. He had every intention of killing that show girl when she got away from him."

"I never said it wasn't murder. I just meant it didn't need to happen. There was no reason for it. No saloon fight, or gambling argument."

"He was after that show girl. Maybe he was going to hold her for ransom, or rape her. Who knows."

"Well, whatever his reason, it doesn't matter. I sent the telegram to the justice this morning. I'll let you know as soon as I have a trial date. You and Bert will have to take him by wagon transport to Red Rock. You'll both be witnesses as well."

"I look forward to watching him hang."

"I'm glad you didn't shoot him," the mayor laughed.

"Don't think it didn't cross my mind."

"Oh, I'm sure it did." He grinned. "Tobias's service will be tomorrow, just after sunrise," he stated, changing the subject.

"Bert and I will be there."

***

When Jessie left his office, she headed to the Fashionette to replace her coat with a new one.

Ike already had a coat ready for her since he'd made an extra suit in her size to keep on hand.

"I still can't believe Tobias is gone," he murmured while ringing up Jessie's purchase in the register.

"The funeral is tomorrow—"

"Yeah, I know," he said. "I'm sure the whole town will be there."

"Probably so."

"Did you hear the Bennett Sisters left on the first stage out of here this morning?"

Jessie nodded, handing him a half eagle coin. "They moved their show over to Red Rock. They have to testify in the trial anyway, so it makes sense."

"Are you sure you don't want a new shirt?" he asked. "I may have one that will fit you."

"No. I still have this one," she replied, indicating the shirt she was wearing as she slipped the new coat on.

"Check with Mrs. Fray at the General Trade. She may have something that will get the stains out of the sleeves on your other shirt."

"I'll do that. Thanks, Ike."

Jessie stepped out of the store and felt the sunlight start to warm her back. She wasn't sure she would be wearing the new coat much longer. Spring was nearly over, and the hot summer would be along soon.

Walking past the theatre, which sat between the Fashionette and General Trade, Jessie saw the wooden sign attached to the double entrance door of Pearl Hall. It simply read: CLOSED. Her jaw tightened, thinking about what had transpired the night before. She blew out a deep sigh of frustration and continued her pace, stepping inside the open doorway of the General Trade.

"Mrs. Fray…" she called, looking around for the woman.

"I'm back here, and my name is Ellie," she scolded, standing up behind the counter, where she had been putting stuff on one of the lower shelves. "Well, if it isn't our town marshal." She shook her head. "Does trouble always follow you, or is it you who goes looking for *it*?"

"We seem to cross paths from time to time," Jessie mumbled.

"It sounds to me like you're trying to get yourself killed…with the way you handled 'High Card' Jack, and now, you have the leader of the Dirty Boys Gang locked up." She crossed her arms.

"Why do you care?"

"I don't," Ellie huffed as she moved out from behind the register to stock more shelves.

Jessie read the back of the soap flakes container, then moved onto the shampoo bottle, looking for something that would remove the stains in her shirt. "Sounds to me like you do," she muttered.

"You've been in here twice in the two months that you've been in town. You know nothing about me."

"You seem to know about me," Jessie replied.

"The whole town knows about you!"

"And that bothers you, Mrs. Fray?"

"Of course not. Why would it? And stop calling me Mrs. Fray. I've told you, my name is Ellie."

"It's customary to call a widow by her married name."

"For the first year, yes. My husband died fifteen months ago, right there on that very street, in fact. All because of the same cruel behavior that took Tobias's life," she said, grabbing the ladder and moving to a different shelf.

"It seems to me that you of all people would want the town cleaned up."

"Tangling with those outlaws only makes it worse. They'll be back, causing twice as much ruckus as they did the first time, and call it revenge. It never ends, Marshal Henry. Don't you see that? They just don't stop. Outlaws are nothing but scum. As far as I'm concerned, they all deserve to be in Boot Hill!"

"It's my job to stop them...no matter what it takes."

"And putting the town folks lives at risk to do it...that's okay to you?"

Jessie opened her mouth to reply, but Ellie lost her footing on the ladder, and fell off the last step, tumbling right into Jessie's arms. Their eyes locked with their faces only a few inches apart.

Ellie tried to pull away, but she was glued to the captivating green eyes staring back at her. Heavy footsteps on the sidewalk outside drew her attention. She backed away quickly, straightening her apron.

Jessie left without making a purchase, while Ellie assisted her new customer.

***

The following day, the town folk gathered in and around the church as the sun began to rise over the mountains. Pastor Noah read a couple of passages from the bible while standing at the pulpit. Then, he moved to the side, placing his hand on the wooden coffin.

"Tobias Freemont was more than a simple man. He was candid. He was smart. At times, he was even funny. But, most of all, he was a dreamer. To him, those stage shows were everything. His whole life revolved around Pearl Hall. Some would call it fitting that he took his last breath on the very stage where he worked day and night, but I would say otherwise. In fact, if he were here right now, he'd say 'Pastor Noah, I'm gonna die someday doing something I hate, like riding a horse, because there is no way God will interrupt me when I'm working.'"

The congregation laughed, knowing that sounded a lot like the theatre manager.

"Well, my brother, my friend, maybe God was ready for you to manage a show full of angels." He stepped back to the pulpit. "Anyway, we're here today to celebrate a life that was tragically cut short, but know this...God has a plan. He has one for each and every one of you. You may not like his plan, in fact you may completely disagree with it, but there's nothing you can do about it. You are put here with one purpose, and one purpose only...to live life. Tobias Freemont lived his life. In fact, he lived it to the fullest every day, doing what he loved to do. So, don't be sad because his life ended...you can be sad because you'll miss him, of course...but be happy. He did exactly what he was put here to do."

Everyone bowed their heads as he said a final prayer, then they filed out of the small building as the pall-bearers walked to the front.

Jessie stood outside during the service with several other people who either couldn't find a seat, or like her, weren't keen on religion.

When they were ready, the pall-bearers lifted the coffin and began the slow walk down the center of Main Street, towards the cemetery. Town folk lined both sides of the path from the church, all the way to the graveyard entrance.

Mayor Montgomery, Jessie, Bert, and Pastor Noah walked side by side behind the six men who carried the coffin. Tobias didn't have any family, but he and Howard Johannes, the owner of Pearl Hall, and one of the pall-bearers in front of them, were very close. He'd been over in Red Rock the night of the shooting, trying to schedule more traveling shows to come to Boone Creek.

Jessie held her head high with her eyes looking straight ahead as she maintained the slow, steady pace, hoping this was the last time she'd ever have to take this walk. As they passed by the General Trade, she couldn't help scanning the crowd. Her breathing stilled when her eyes landed on Ellie, wearing a black dress suit with a matching bonnet on her head. Her cheeks were red and she held a handkerchief up, drying her tears as they fell.

ELEVEN

It had been a few days since Tobias was laid to rest. The town of Boone Creek had gone back to normal, despite the theatre still being closed. Howard didn't have plans to reopen. In fact, he'd sent a telegram to several cities, claiming the business for sale. No one wanted to see him leave, but with Tobias gone and the tragedy that had unfolded on that stage, he simply had no reason to ever go back inside. Thus, giving him no reason to stay in town.

"Have you heard anything from the mayor?" Bert asked, taking a seat beside Jessie, at the bar in the Rustler's Den Saloon.

"Still no word on the trial date. He says any day now," she answered, sipping a cup of coffee.

"I'm not sure how much more of Shamus's mouth I can take. I'm liable to get a bottle of opium from Doc Vernon and put it in his food."

Jessie grinned. "He's full of penniless threats. Don't let him get to you."

"How come it's not bothering you, what he's saying?"

"Honestly, I think about something else. It's the only thing that keeps me from putting a hole clean through his forehead."

Bert grimaced at the visual. "You're not worried any of it might be true?"

"Do I look worried?"

"No."

"Are you?"

"No…yes. Maybe."

"Good. You can worry for the both of us, then." She patted him on the shoulder and waved Elmer over. "If his friends show up, they show up. You can shoot a gun, now. Remember?"

"Can I get you something, Deputy Bert?"

"No, I'm good. Thank you."

"Hey, Elmer, do you ever get stains on your shirt sleeves?" Jessie asked.

"Oh, I used to. Coffee, cigar ashes, red wine, you name it. They all stain."

"How did you get the stains out?"

"I didn't. I bought a new shirt every time, until I got a pair of these," he said, pointing to the black sleeve covers he was wearing. "Have you checked the General Trade? Ms. Ellie might have something that will work."

"Yeah, she hates me," she mumbled inaudibly. "I guess I'll give it another try."

***

Ellie was finishing up with a customer when Jessie walked in. Their eyes met briefly before Ellie pulled away. "What can I help you with, Marshal?"

"I've been told you might have what I'm looking for," Jessie said, moseying over to the counter where Ellie was standing.

"And what might that be?"

"Stain-removing soap flakes."

Ellie raised a brow.

Boone Creek

"I have a shirt with stains on it. I'm trying to get them out."

"What kind of stains?"

"Blood," Jessie answered.

"From the shooting," Ellie murmured, mostly to herself. However, Jessie heard her and nodded. "I'm not sure what, if anything, would work on that."

"It was worth a shot. I guess I'll toss it out and purchase a new one."

"Is this why you were in here the other day?"

"Yes."

"I didn't get to say thank you...for not letting me fall on my backside," she said, fighting the smile that was trying to form on her mouth.

The corner of Jessie's mouth turned up in a half grin.

"Good afternoon, Pastor Noah," Ellie said, cheerfully greeting her newest patron.

"Pastor," Jessie obliged, tipping her hat.

"Marshal," he replied, doing the same. "I didn't see you grace us with your presence inside the church at Mr. Freemont's service. Deputy Bert and his lovely Molly, were on the second row, as they are every Sunday, so God obviously doesn't have it out for lawmen and ladies."

"Oh, I'm sure he doesn't, but I'm not interested in taking my chances," she said.

"Ms. Ellie here, goes as well. Although, she usually sits near the back." He smiled.

"Haven't missed a service in nearly two years," Ellie replied.

"Well, then. I should probably get back to Bert. Our prisoner is keeping him on edge," Jessie said, turning to leave.

74

"Any word on when the trial will be?"

"Not yet. Soon I hope," she said over her shoulder, just before walking outside.

***

"Clocks ticking, Marshal," Shamus said. From his cell, he had an impartial view of Jessie sitting at her desk.

"Sure is," she replied, sorting through the Wanted posters.

"The mayor just got a telegram. Looks like we might have a trial date," Bert exclaimed, rushing inside the small building.

"How do you know that?"

"I was just at the post. My cousin Grim sent me a telegram from San Francisco."

"What does that have to do with the mayor and the trial?"

"A telegram came in for him from the territory justice in Red Rock, while I was there. I heard them send for him."

"Well, well, well. Looks like we're taking a trip. Just the three of us," Shamus sneered. "I wonder how far you'll actually get. I know it won't be anywhere near Red Rock."

"Shamus, Bert's going to shoot you if you don't be quiet. Then, nobody will be going anywhere, except you...to Boot Hill, where you belong. Now, shut up!" Jessie growled. "Keep an eye on that buffoon. I'll be back in a bit," she said to Bert.

"Good news," Mayor Montgomery stated, meeting Jessie in the street when she left the Marshal's Office.

"I heard. Do we have a date?"

"Three weeks from today."

Jessie shook her head. "Three days would've been better."

"I agree, but at least it's moving forward," he said.

Jessie noticed Ellie across the way, sweeping the daily street dust from her store's floor, all the while, keeping an eye on them. When the mayor headed off towards his office, Jessie meandered the rest of the way over to the General Trade.

"Marshal Henry," Ellie greeted. "Twice in one day," she added as she strolled from one side of the store to the other, making room for some new products she'd taken in trade. She was dressed in a black walking-skirt and paisley shirt with a white apron around her waist, similar to what she wore every day. But today her skirt seemed to flow around her ankles as she moved, almost like she was hovering just above the floor.

Jessie tipped her hat and pulled her eyes away. She'd gone into the store simply because Ellie had been watching her, but nonetheless, she needed more kerosene for the jailhouse lamp, which she'd forgotten to get earlier that day. Otherwise, their prisoner would be spending the night in the dark.

"I have some new tea leaves, took them in on trade a bit ago. They're mint flavored," Ellie said.

"I'm afraid I have no way of preparing them where I board."

"I just made a fresh pot upstairs. Would you like to try it?"

"Uh...sure. I'd love to."

"I'll be right down," Ellie said, heading up the iron, spiraled staircase that led to her room on the second floor of the building.

Jessie grabbed the jars of kerosene that she'd come for and set them on the counter, where she waited for Ellie to return. She removed her hat and swallowed the lump forming in her throat. She'd never been invited for tea, and wasn't sure of the proper etiquette. "Here, let me help you with that," she said, moving to assist as Ellie walked down the stairs carrying a tea pot in one hand, and a stack of cups in the other.

"It's quite all right," Ellie replied, stepping carefully off the last step.

Jessie remained close by in case she had another incident.

"I believe you're supposed to drink it as is, but I'm sure a drop of milk would be fine. However, I don't think sugar goes well with mint," Ellie explained, filling two of the cups.

"I'm fine with it like this." Jessie picked up one of the cups.

"Where did you say you were from?" Ellie asked, taking a small sip.

"The south," Jessie answered, taking a large, nervous swallow. She coughed a few times, trying to breathe while her throat burned. "That's some strong stuff," she mumbled.

Ellie laughed. "Well, that's because you're supposed to sip it, not chug it like a glass of whiskey."

Jessie only nodded. It was the first time she'd ever heard Ellie laugh, or seen her smile for that matter. The sound of her laughter was endearing, and the smile on her face made her appear much softer than the hard-edged, young woman Jessie had first met. If it wasn't for the aroma of the tea tickling her senses, she would've forgotten to breathe. Taking a much smaller sip, she savored the flavor.

Noticing her enjoyment, Ellie said, "See, it's not bad when you drink it properly."

"I agree." She grinned.

"The south is pretty large," Ellie muttered.

"So is the state of Texas," Jessie said. "What about you? Where are you from?"

"A small town outside of Dodge City."

Jessie nodded. "I've been to Kansas...never made it to Dodge, though."

"Well..." Ellie cleared her throat. "I should probably get these rung up for you," Ellie stated, grabbing the two jars and moving over to the register. "Didn't you just come in for kerosene?"

"The inside of the jail has to be lit up at night when we have someone locked up. Otherwise, he'd be in complete darkness from sun down to sun up. Thankfully, he's only here for a few more weeks. His trial date has been set." Jessie pulled a couple of trade dollars from her vest pocket, setting them on the counter before slipping her hat back on. "Add a tin of these tea leaves, too. Please."

"I thought you said you couldn't make it."

"I can't, but I know someone who can. I think she'll like it."

TWELVE

The next evening, Jessie found herself in the middle of another saloon fight at the Rustler's Den. They seemed to be becoming nightly occurrences. She and Bert stood no chance against the four men as they tussled in the street. Thankfully, none of them was wearing a gun belt.

"Break it up!" Bert yelled.

Jessie had finally had enough, especially when she noticed one of the men had a pistol tucked into his pants under his vest. She drew her pistol, firing a warning shot into the air. "Damn it! You're going to all calm down, or you can spend the night in the jail!" she shouted, putting her gun back in the holster. "I don't care who started it or what you were fighting over to begin with. It's done. It ends here. Call it a night and go home."

"You pansy-ass law lady can't tell me what to do," one of the men slurred.

"As the Town Marshal, I damn sure can. Now, get moving!" she growled, placing her hands on her gun belt.

Bert saw one of the other men move, but before he could say anything, the man reached for the gun under his vest. Jessie saw his shadow waver on the ground in the lamp lighting and spun around with her hand on the butt of her pistol.

"I'll shoot your hand right off your arm before you ever get to it, so don't even think about it."

"You don't scare me," he sneered.

Jessie laughed, "If you scare me, I'm in the wrong line of work."

"The hell with this. Come on, Billy," one of the men called as he walked over to where his horse was tied up. The other two men also decided to leave.

"Listen to your friend. I'm giving you a free pass to leave without any trouble. Otherwise, you're looking at a night in jail for drunkenness and fighting, plus a fine for carrying a gun in town."

"I don't need to listen to no body," he spat.

Jessie watched his hand quiver slightly.

"You leave me no choice," she said, raising her arm up with lightning speed. "Bang!" she shouted.

The guy lurched back, falling to the ground as the horse nearby rose up on his hind legs, whinnying. Everything had happened so fast, no one noticed Jessie's hand was shaped like a gun and her pistol was still in the holster. Bert stared in disbelief.

"Get your ass up and get out of my town," Jessie growled through gritted teeth.

A wet spot appeared on the dirt in the street when the man stood up. He said nothing as he got on his horse and rode off with his friend. The other two men were already long gone.

"He pissed himself," Bert muttered, still in shock.

"He was scared. I knew he wasn't going to shoot to me."

"How did you know?"

"His hand wasn't steady enough to even try to draw. His shadow shook like a flickering candle."

"Come on, this rounds on me," Jessie said, leading him back into the saloon.

"I don't drink, remember?"

Jessie vaguely recalled him mentioning something of the sort. "Not at all?" she asked.

"Well, no."

"You don't drink, you don't smoke, you've never been inside a brothel..." Jessie raised a brow. "Bert, do you have a penis?"

"I beg your pardon," he said, looking appalled. "Of course. Why would you ask such a thing?"

"I'm just making sure you're really a man." She shrugged. "I drink, I smoke, I live in a brothel...but I definitely do not have a penis."

"Will you stop talking about penises if I have a drink?"

"Absolutely." She waved Elmer over. "Get us a round. Bert has found his penis. He's officially a man!"

Elmer laughed.

"For crying out loud. You're as bad as the rest of the heathens in here," Bert uttered.

"Oh, loosen your corset and have a drink. It tastes horrible, no offense, Elmer..."

"None taken," he replied, setting the two glasses in front of them.

"But, it won't kill you," she finished.

"Why are we doing this again?" Bert asked, picking up the glass.

"Because we are thankful that drunken fool didn't draw that pistol and try to shoot at either of us. Plus, he pissed himself, so that's a bonus."

Bert nodded and knocked the glass back, swallowing the liquor in one big gulp. "Holy hell!" he yelped, rubbing his chest with his free hand as he sat the glass down. "That burns!"

Jessie and Elmer laughed.

***

After a second glass, Bert was done for. Jessie threw his arm around her neck and helped him out of the saloon. "I said *a* drink, Bert. Not half the damn bottle," she huffed. "Where the hell do you live anyway?"

"Molly and I rent a house over behind the corral near Pinewood Pass," he said, mentioning the other road leading out of town. It was near the mayor's office, and circled around towards Pinewood Valley, which was a flat area behind Boone Mountain, but also had a cattle trail cutoff just outside of Boone Creek.

"How come I didn't know that?" she asked as they walked down Center Street.

"We never talked about it, I guess," he slurred slightly. "You're the best town marshal in the territory."

"Thanks," she said.

"But, you scare the hell out of me, sometimes."

"That's...good to know...I think." She paused, looking at the row of houses. Only two of them were dimly lit, the rest were dark. "Which one is yours?"

"In the middle," he mumbled, pointing to one of the lit ones.

Jessie helped him up the couple of stairs, which sounded more like a pair of elephants. The door swung open before Jessie could knock, and a petite woman wearing night clothes appeared, holding a lantern that was used as a hanging lamp. Her reddish-brown hair hung down her front right side in a thick braid.

"Bert? Good, lord. What's happened to you?" she gasped, holding the light up.

"He had a little too much to drink."

"What? He doesn't drink."

"Oh, no..." Bert murmured. "Here it comes."

"Quick, get him off the steps!" the woman yelled. Jessie rushed him back down to the street just before he began heaving all over the ground, narrowly missing Jessie's leg.

"He doesn't drink because he gets sick," the woman said, holding the lantern towards the two of them. "Marshal Henry?"

"Yes, ma'am. You must be Molly."

"I am."

"I apologize for us meeting like this."

"I've seen you before, around town. Several times, actually. I've told Bert to invite you for supper, but he likes to keep home and work separate."

"With the thugs running ramped around here, I don't blame him. He's a good man."

"He's also a very stubborn man. How in the world did you get him to drink?"

Jessie bit her lower lip, feeling a little shameful. "I questioned his manhood."

"My word," she giggled. "No wonder he drank."

"Never again," Bert croaked, after puking two more times.

"I'll be right back. Let me get him some water."

Jessie gazed up at the stars. For a split second, her mind drifted to Ellie, but Molly returned quickly, handing her a glass of well water from the pump, which she gave to Bert.

"I have it from here. He'll wake up feeling pretty rough in the morning, but he'll be fine."

"This has happened before?"

"Yes. He got into the whiskey one other time with his cousin Grimsby. It wasn't pretty," she explained. "The doctor said his stomach just couldn't handle it, and told him it was best to never do it again."

"Should I go get Doc Vernon?"

"Oh, no. He'll be fine."

"Okay." Jessie nodded. "It was nice meeting you."

"You as well, Marshal Henry. Maybe supper is a better idea, next time."

Jessie smiled.

***

Around noon the next day, Jessie sat at a table in the Kettle Kitchen, drinking a cup of coffee and eating chicken pot pie, which was pretty much her breakfast since she hadn't been up more than two hours.

"I heard it was a rough night," the waitress said, refilling her coffee.

"No rougher than any other, really."

"Personally, I'm glad you're cleaning up our town. Marshal Milford, may he rest in peace, wasn't much on law and order. Don't get me wrong, he did his best to keep the peace, but in doing so, he pretty much let them outlaws, drunkards, and whoever else caused a ruckus, do whatever they wanted around here."

The corner of Jessie's mouth turned up in a grin as she pushed her empty plate aside.

"I won't ask you how your meal was. You come here every day, so you must like our cooking," the waitress said with a big smile.

Jessie laughed. "Do you think I could get a piece of that brandied peach pie to go?"

Graysen Morgen

"Of course you can. I'll be right back."

Jessie placed forty cents on the table to cover her bill and pulled the watch from her vest pocket to check the time. When the waitress returned with the pie wrapped in a cloth napkin, Jessie thanked her and slipped her hat back on as she headed out.

***

Bert didn't have a desk in the Marshal's Office, but he borrowed Jessie's from time to time. As he sat down in the rickety chair to eat the lunch Molly had packed him, the sweet smell of peaches permeated the air. He took a peek under the napkin sitting nearby.

"That's not for you!" Jessie barked, snatching the napkin-covered pie off the desk. "I'll be back," she said.

"Is that for Miss Ellie?" he asked.

Jessie didn't answer.

"You're sweet on her, aren't you?"

"What?"

"It's all right, if you are. I'm sure you're not sweet on any of the men around here."

"It's nothing. She made some tea yesterday, so—"

"She invited you for tea?" He crossed his arms and smiled. "She must be sweet on you, too. Who would've thought—"

"Bert, if you don't want to spend another night retching all over yourself, you'll stop right there and eat your damn lunch." She turned back towards the door. "It smells good, by the way."

"Leftover beef steak with onions," he called as she headed across the street with the pie in her hand.

85

Ellie was standing behind the counter, writing a list on a piece of paper, when Jessie walked in. "Marshal." She nodded with a smile. "What brings you in?"

"Brandied peach pie," Jessie said, placing the napkin on the counter. "I thought you could use a treat. Well, after going through the trouble of making the tea, and all," Jessie stammered.

The sweet aroma from the dessert made Ellie's stomach rumble as she uncovered it. "This smells absolutely divine."

"I'm sure it tastes just as good."

"You haven't tried it?"

"No."

"I'll be right back." Ellie disappeared up the stairs, returning a moment later with two forks. "You simply must share it with me," she said. "Besides, I made that pot of tea for all of my customers to try, hoping they'd buy a tin of leaves."

Jessie nodded, unsure of what to say as she removed her hat.

Ellie handed her a fork. "Are you really from Texas?" she asked.

Jessie nodded.

"Were you a law officer down there, too?" Ellie questioned between bites of pie.

"Oh...no." Jessie shook her head. "I ran cattle across the Texas and Mexico border."

Ellie raised a brow.

"What? You can't picture me as a cow poke?" Jessie's mouth turned up into a slight grin.

"Something like that." Ellie smiled. "What brought you to Boone Creek?"

"The chance at a different life. What about you? Why did you leave...Dodge City, was it?"

"Near there," Ellie said. "I came here with my husband. He had this big idea for a trade store out west. We passed through here and decided to settle."

Jessie nodded, looking at Ellie as she went in for another bite of pie. Their forks touched in the center of the last piece. They smiled at each other and Jessie pulled her fork away, allowing Ellie to have the last morsel. However, she sliced it in half, allowing them to share it.

"That was delicious," Ellie said, placing her fork on the empty napkin. "Thank you."

"You're quite welcome, even if you didn't make the tea for me," Jessie teased.

"Well, you were the first person I served it to. Does that matter?"

Jessie grinned. "Maybe."

"If I didn't know any better, I'd say you were courting me, Marshal Henry."

"Me...courting you? Oh, no. I believe it's the other way around, Ms. Ellie."

"How so?" Ellie asked, crossing her arms. "You're the one who has been in here three times this week, and brought me pie."

"You made me tea...before everyone else, and I see you looking over at my office nearly every day."

Ellie huffed. "What makes you think I'd be sweet on another woman?"

Jessie stepped closer, leaving less than a foot of space between them. "Because I can see it in your eyes," she whispered, before turning around and walking away.

THIRTEEN

Nicolas Munroe, a potential buyer for Pearl Hall, arrived in town a few days later in a fancy stage. He was the epitome of wealth, with a thin, handle-bar mustache, and high-fashioned suits with colorful vests and ties, and a top hat. He would've somewhat fit in with the business people of Red Rock, and especially in Denver, the largest city in the territory, but in Boone Creek, he stood out like a horse in a dress.

He carried on about his travels and boasted about the money he'd made, owning various businesses, to anyone who would listen. He'd never owned a theatre, but to him, it was simply another way to line his pocket. Many of the other business owners were partial to him already, believing he would boost the economy in the town, but Jessie likened him to a snake oil salesman.

***

Jessie and Bert walked into the Rustler's Den, per their usual evening patrol around town. Elmer waved and Jessie tipped her hat.

"Well, what do we have here?" Nicolas Munroe said, looking at the two of them. He was in the middle of a game of dice, with nearly everyone in the saloon watching. "You must be the town marshal I keep hearing about," he added. "Care to join in?"

"Maybe later," Jessie replied, passing by him to go to their usual table in the back corner.

Bert had sworn off whiskey for the rest of his life, and they were working, so Elmer sent over two hot cups of coffee.

"I knew it wouldn't be long before you walked in," Lita said as she sauntered over, hiking her hip onto the edge of the table.

Bert pulled his eyes away from the ample bosom spilling over the top of her corset.

"Is he any good?" Jessie asked, nodding towards Mr. Munroe, who seemed to be winning the game.

"No one is as good as you," she uttered, running her hand down Jessie's arm.

Jessie ignored the advance and sipped her coffee.

"Why don't you give it a shot? He's beaten nearly everyone in here," Lita stated.

"How many games has he won?" she asked.

"Oh, I don't know, maybe ten."

"In a row?" Bert asked.

"The good deputy speaks," she teased, winking at him.

Bert cringed nervously.

"Yes, ten in a row. He's been here for about an hour."

"I'll be right back," Jessie said, getting up from the table.

Bert watched her walk away, anything to keep from looking at the enticing saloon girl. Lita opened her mouth to say something and he quickly blurted, "I'm a married man."

Lita laughed. "So are most of the men in here."

Jessie took a seat at the bar and lit a cigar. Elmer noticed her and made his way towards that end.

"Whiskey?" he asked.

"No, I need to keep my head on straight tonight. How long has he been at it?" she asked, nodding towards the dice table.

"You think he's running a game?"

"Lita told me he's won ten straight, been here an hour or so."

"Yeah." Elmer nodded.

"You ever see anyone win like that?"

He didn't have to think about it, he simply shook his head. "Damn it. I liked him, too."

"I can't prove he's running a game, but I can smell a rat from a mile away, and he stinks."

Elmer pulled several quarters out of the register. "Here, he wants you to play. He keeps watching you."

"I'm not playing with house money."

"Why?" Elmer questioned. "Are you going to lose?"

Jessie never backed down when she was challenged. She grabbed the coins, putting them in the vest pocket opposite her own money, and made her way to the table.

Nicolas had taken off his hat and coat, leaving him in the gray pants of his suit, along with a white shirt, and bright blue matching vest and puff tie. His brown hair was waxed and perfectly combed, as was his mustache.

"Excuse me, folks. Let the good marshal get in here," he said, making room for Jessie at the table.

All of the seats were taken, but she preferred to stand anyhow. The rules were simple, the castor rolled the dice, and he called the main before each roll, which was a total number when the dice was rolled. Anything can be called except seven or eleven, which was called a hitch. Betting was easy. You either bet that he would roll a hitch, or bet on specific numbers other than the main, or bet that the number would be odd or even. If the castor rolled the main, he won the entire pot. If he rolled a hitch, seven or eleven, he won half the pot. If he rolled any other number, the pot was won by whoever had that number. Those who played odd or even only won when the castor lost, and they were paid one to one odds. The castor remained the same person until he lost three in a row.

Nicolas called a nine, and Jessie put a quarter on the hitch circle. The dice bounced down the board and off the side wall, landing on five and four, giving him the full pot. Again, Nicolas called the main. This time it was six. He rolled a seven, giving him half of the pot. Jessie had played nine. She reached in for the dice, to be helpful and hand them to Nicolas, but he'd already retrieved them with the L-shaped stick that was used for that purpose. He smiled and called another main to keep the game going.

"You guys are too good for me," Jessie joked, walking away after losing five straight rolls. She headed back over to Elmer, slipping him the rest of the coins he'd loaned her.

"Well?" he said.

"He's not using house dice. He switched them."

"What do you mean?"

"They're weighted, so he knows the numbers they will land on."

"How did he switch them?"

"Sleight of hand. It's rather easy," she said, not going into too much detail. It was a trick she'd used several times over the years to gain a little money when she gambled. Nicolas was playing like a fool, however. He'd won too much, too fast, giving him away.

"That cheating son of a bitch. I want him out of here."

Jessie held her hand up in a calming manner. "Let him play his game tonight and think he has everyone beaten. I'll bust him next time."

"It's your call, Marshal."

Jessie handed him a half eagle. "That's how much I lost."

"He's making a killing over there. Do you think he'll try it again?"

"If he's smart, no. But, I don't give him much credit," Jessie replied, looking back at the table.

"Someone's liable to catch on and shoot him," Elmer said.

"No one is carrying, at least not that I can see. That's one problem we've just about gotten control of. It's the ones who conceal it that we have to worry about." She turned back to Elmer. "My coffee's getting cold," she said, tipping her hat to him before walking back to Bert.

Lita had vacated her spot when Jessie went to the dice table, following to stand alongside her. They'd parted when Jessie went back up to the bar.

"What's going on?" Bert asked.

"Our new visitor is running a game at the dice table."

"What are we going to do about it?"

"Nothing…at least for now. He'll do it again. He's as slick as a snake oil salesman." She took a sip of her cold coffee. "Come on, let's call it a night."

"What if someone else catches onto what he's doing?" Bert asked as they left.

She shrugged. "Then, it serves him right for trying to hustle everyone."

***

"Will you save me some honey?" Jessie yelled to Ellie, who was standing on the sidewalk in front of her store, updating the chalkboard sign out front with all of her weekly and daily specials. "The last time you put it on sale, you sold out within two days."

"Well, come buy some, then," Ellie called back, placing a hand on her slender hip.

"Bert, hold down the fort. I'll be right back," Jessie said, popping her head inside the opened doorway.

"You should try flowers this time. That worked on my Molly."

"Bert..." Jessie stared at him. "Never mind," she muttered, walking away.

"I can't get it now because I'm not sure how long I'll be gone. We leave for Red Rock in a couple of days for Shamus's trial."

"Oh," Ellie mumbled. "This stuff's no good anyway. That's why I have it on sale. The last batch was better. In fact, I mixed it with homemade jam Mrs. Porter made. It's very good on a biscuit."

"Sounds like I might have to try that some time."

"I always bake too many biscuits for just me. I'll go get you one."

Jessie smiled, but Ellie had already headed inside. She nodded hello to a few town folk who passed by while she waited.

"Here, you are," Ellie said, handing her the biscuit, covered in the honey and jam mixture. It was wrapped in the cloth napkin from the restaurant.

"I'd forgotten about this. Ms. Nelly over at the Kettle Kitchen is probably wondering why I haven't brought it back."

"Did she ask you for it?"

"No."

"That means she's not missing it."

"You didn't have to do this," Jessie said, taking a bite of the biscuit. "Oh, my. This *is* good."

"Thank you, and I only did it to repay you for bringing me the pie."

Jessie met her eyes and simply stared.

"You look deep in thought," Ellie murmured.

"I was," Jessie said shyly, pulling her eyes away and finishing her biscuit.

"What were you thinking about?"

Jessie shook her head. "You have a nice afternoon, Miss Ellie." She turned to go.

"Wait...you're not going to tell me?" She reached out for Jessie's arm, but wound up grabbing her hand.

Jessie looked down at their paired hands. "Do you really want to know?"

Ellie quickly let go of her hand and went back inside of the store.

Jessie sighed as she walked across the street to the Marshal's Office. She was barely in the door when Ellie hurried in behind her.

"Marshal, you dropped the napkin. Ms. Nelly might be needing that back."

"Ohhhweee, would you look at that!" Shamus exclaimed. "You sure are a pretty thing!"

Ellie cringed.

"He's all bark and no bite, trust me," Jessie said, walking her out. "Thank you for bringing over the napkin."

"You're welcome," she said, taking a long look at Jessie's bright green eyes. "You look lost in thought again. What is it?"

"Maybe I'll tell you when I get back," Jessie mumbled, thinking about the same thing that had been on her mind minutes earlier.

"Your eyes already told me," Ellie said softly.

"Hey, that's my line."

"Well, I borrowed it."

"Fine. What did they say?" Jessie asked, resting her hands on her gun belt.

"Oh...maybe I'll tell you when you get back," Ellie teased.

Jessie simply shook her head and grinned as Ellie headed back across the street.

"I might have to come back to town for that little lady," Shamus said when Jessie stepped back inside.

She walked over to his cell and grabbed the front of his shirt collar in a bunch, pulling his face against the iron bars. "You come near her, and I'll skin you alive," she growled through gritted teeth. "Besides, the only way you're coming back here is as a ghost. I plan to witness the executioner snap your neck like a twig."

Bert silently watched the exchange. Jessie Henry was fierce and confident, definitely unlike any lawman he'd ever seen. He admired her in a lot of ways.

"I told you to try flowers," he said as she stepped back over to her desk.

Graysen Morgen

"If you don't stop, I'm going to put you in there with him," she muttered.

FOURTEEN

Jessie saw Lita coming out of the General Trade as she passed her on the street. Lita smiled and waved, and Jessie tipped her hat as she kept going in the direction of the mayor's office.

"Marshal Henry!" Pastor Noah yelled, seeing her pass by as he stood at the pulpit, working on his sermon for Sunday.

Hearing her name, Jessie stopped. "What can I do for you?" she asked as he walked outside.

"It's a beautiful day, isn't it?" he said, looking up at the blue, cloudless sky.

"Sure is."

"Say, what do you know about scripture?"

"About as much as you know about skinning a buffalo."

Pastor Noah laughed.

"Have you ever heard of Hebrews 11:1 'Faith is confidence in what we hope for and assurance about what we do not see.'"

"How does that pertain to me, exactly?"

"You and Bert have a big job ahead of you. Trust that everything will go all right and guarantee that it won't."

Jessie pursed her lips and nodded. "When you put it like that, it makes sense."

The pastor smiled.

"Let me ask you something. Why bother watching over someone like me who isn't a churchgoer?"

"That's simple. Romans 14:1 'Accept the one whose faith is weak, without quarrelling over disputable matters,'" he said. "You may not come to church, but it doesn't mean I condemn you for it. I'm not God. I merely deliver his word, and everyone is permitted to receive the word of God. You don't have to sit in a church for that. Besides...I like you."

"It's good to know you're on my side. Maybe you could put in a good word for me from time to time," she said, pointing to the sky.

"Every Sunday," he replied. "If I don't see you before you leave, safe travels to you and Bert. I'll be praying for you."

***

"Make sure you have enough provisions," Mayor Montgomery said. "It's a two-day ride to Red Rock. I have you and Bert booked at the Silver Penny Hotel for the length of the trial. When you get into town, go directly to the jailhouse and get Shamus checked in. It's next door to the justice's office. He should be able to help you if you have any questions."

"We'll be fine," Jessie replied, sitting across from him in his office. "I should probably pick up a few things before we head out, though. I want to leave at first light."

"Get whatever you need and put it on my bill at the General Trade."

"Are you sure you'll be able to keep an eye on the streets while we're gone? It might be easier to deputize someone until we get back."

"I'll be all right. I'm more worried about the two of you."

"I'm not scared of that loudmouth or his gang of nitwits," Jessie stated.

"I think that's what worries me." The mayor grinned.

***

Jessie headed to the General Trade after leaving the mayor's office. She'd decided to go ahead and pick up the few items they needed for the trip.

"Marshal," Ellie uttered when Jessie walked in.

"We meet again," Nicolas Munroe said.

"Well, Mr. Munroe, it's not that big of a town," she replied with a hint of sarcasm. She was slightly surprised to see him, especially looking so casual as he leaned against the counter.

"That's true, but the new, improved theatre will put this town on the map when I buy it."

"So, you *are* going to buy it then?"

"I haven't decided, but Ms. Ellie has all but talked me into it. I think she'd make a great business neighbor. What do you think, Marshal?"

"If you have the money, then why talk about it? Just do it," she said, grabbing some candles, matches, and dry food goods.

"Oh, now that's easier said than done, I'm afraid. These business transactions take time. I need to be sure I'm making the right investment before I get things started." He looked at Ellie and grinned like a Cheshire cat. "Although, I do believe this could be my best acquirement yet."

Ellie smiled.

Jessie put her items on the counter next to Nicolas.

"I don't believe I caught your name the other night. Those games did go rather quickly," he smirked.

Jessie didn't look the least bit amused by him. "Jessie Henry, Town Marshal," she said, holding her hand out.

His brow furrowed as he shook hands with her. "Henry...I met a guy named Jed Henry when I was in North Carolina. He fought in the war. Is he any relation to you?"

Jessie shook her head. "No. My Pa's name was Johnny. He followed the gold rush to California when I was little and died before he made it back home."

"My apologies."

"Don't fret. I never knew him anyway," she uttered.

"Well, excuse me anyhow. Miss Ellie, it was mighty fine talking with you," he beamed. "Marshal Henry," he added, tipping his gray top hat in her direction, before leaving the store.

Jessie stood impatiently, waiting for Ellie to ring up her purchase. "You two looked pretty chummy."

"What do you mean by that? He's nice, and if we want him to buy the theatre and help our economy, then yes, I'll be friendly," she said, adding Jessie's items in the register. "You don't care for him, do you?"

"Not in the least bit. How could you tell?"

"You were impolite."

"He deserved it."

"Why on earth would you say that?"

"Never mind."

"You sure say that a lot," Ellie retorted.

Jessie shrugged. "The mayor said to put all of this on his bill."

"I don't suppose you brought a sack with you."

"No. I didn't. May I borrow one?"

"Fine," Ellie answered. "By the way, your harlot was in here this morning to get more of the wonderful tea leaves you gave her."

"My what? Wait a second. First of all, I don't have a harlot."

"Everyone has seen you parading around town with her."

"If you're referring to Lita, I know her because we met when I went to Miss Mable's with the mayor to get my room. She's a saloon girl, so I see her at the Rustler's Den when I am working at night. Neither of those is any indication that we are anything but acquaintances."

"Being friendly with her isn't exactly…"

"What? Appropriate?" Jessie shook her head. "And by the way, I gave those tea leaves to Miss Mable to repay her for the hospitality I've been given at her place. She must have made tea for the girls if Lita knew about the leaves."

"Hospitality?" Ellie laughed with a sneer. "You're boarding in a brothel. How hospitable can it be?"

"What is this really about?" Jessie asked.

"You don't care for Mr. Munroe, and I don't care for the harlot," Ellie spat, folding her arms.

"I don't care for Nicolas Munroe because I know his kind. He's as slick as a snake oil salesman, and as broke as a penniless drunk."

"He's barely been here long enough to meet everyone, so I doubt you know much about him."

"You're sweet on him, aren't you?"

"I don't know, but it's of no concern to you."

"You're right, it's not. I guess now I can stop thinking about how wonderful it would be to kiss your lips." Jessie grabbed the sack-full of items and stormed out of the store, leaving Ellie standing behind the counter, slack-jawed.

FIFTEEN

The sky was still dark when Jessie arose and began getting dressed. She'd tried to sleep, but had spent most of the night tossing and turning on edge. She wasn't nervous about the ride to Red Rock with the lawbreaker. In fact, she was more at ease in the open range than anywhere else. No...it was thoughts of Ellie that had kept her awake, more like Ellie and Nicolas. She wondered if she'd be receiving a wedding invite when she returned from the trial. Who knew how long she'd be gone, and he'd more than likely waste no time scheming and conniving until the beautiful store owner was his.

A yawn turned into a long sigh as she finished buttoning her vest and strapping on her gun belt. She spun the cylinder of her Colt Peacemaker pistol, making sure it was fully loaded, before sliding it into the holster. Then, she slipped into her coat and grabbed her hat.

She briefly thought about knocking as she walked past Lita's room, but she didn't want to disturb her if she had company. Instead, she made her way down the stairs and out the front door.

The lights were on at the Rustler's Den, which didn't officially open until ten a.m. She stepped inside, using the back door. "Elmer?" she called, checking to make sure everything was okay.

"Back here!" he yelled, coming out of the storage room.

"It's a little early to be open."

"Oh, I'm not open. I thought you might need this," he replied, handing her a steaming hot pot of coffee.

"Thank you," she said, holding out her hand.

"You be safe out there. Good luck in getting that bastard to hang. I wish I was there to see it myself," he muttered, shaking her hand.

"I'll tell you all about it when I get back."

"I'll save my good bottle, then." He smiled, referring to his best whiskey.

***

The stable was quiet when Jessie walked up, carrying her coffee pot. An open top, four-wheeled wagon was parked on the side with two black horses hitched to it. There was a single seat across the front, and the back had benches on both sides that opened for storage.

"Here you go, Marshal," the stable-hand said, walking out to greet her. "I put the food and water for the horses in the storage under the seat. The rest of the compartments are empty so you can stow your provisions and luggage. There are two candle lanterns under the seat as well. They hang on these hooks right here," he said, pointing to the hook on each end of the seat. "I'll put your coffee pot on the footboard and tie a string around it. That way, you'll be able to get to it without stopping and going into the back."

"Thanks," she replied, climbing up into the seat. "Get a move on," she yelled, seeing Bert walking down the street from his house. He picked up the pace and tossed a picnic basket into the back, before climbing up beside her. "What the hell is that?"

"Molly insisted on sending food."

Jessie grinned. "Is this your first time away from home?"

"First time without her, yes. She's a bit worried."

Jessie nodded and grabbed the reins. She tipped her hat to the stable-hand and slapped the reins on the horses' rear-ends softly to get them moving. The horses lurched forward at an easy trot as she directed them over to the mayor's office up the street. "You stay here," she said, pulling the reins to stop the horses. She set the brake on the wagon and hopped down.

Mayor Montgomery pulled the door open when she knocked. "Here's the stage gun," he said, handing her a sawed-off, double barrel shot gun. "And these are two extra pistols, plus the ammo for everything. Hopefully, you won't need it. When you get into Red Rock, you'll need to check these with the Sheriff. Since you're law enforcement, you'll be permitted to wear your gun belts with one pistol each."

"Okay," she said, taking the shotgun and the canvas sack from him. "I'll wire you when we arrive."

The mayor nodded and shook her hand, before closing the door.

"What's that?" Bert asked.

"It's a shot gun. You do know how to shoot a shot gun, right?" She thought back to when she'd taught him how to actually shoot his pistol. He'd practiced several times on his own and had gotten even better. He was nowhere near the shot that she was, but he could hit a target.

"Yes, of course."

"This will be right here, under your feet," she said, sliding the shotgun into the built in holder. "Here's an extra pistol," she added, pulling both of them from the sack, handing one to him after sticking the other in her gun belt.

Bert took the gun and stuck it through his belt, just as she had done. The bag made a thud sound when she dropped it in the wooden floorboard box next to the coffee pot. Jessie grabbed the reins, released the brake, and directed the horses down the street towards the Marshal's Office, which was around the curve. When they arrived, she set the brake and looped the reins around the footboard.

"Marshal," Ellie called.

Jessie turned to see the General Trade door was open, with Ellie standing nearby.

"Get the paperwork. I'll be back to help you with Shamus in a second."

"Flowers," Bert said loudly as she walked away.

Jessie shook her head and kept going. She stepped inside the store as Ellie held the door open.

"I couldn't let you head out without...well, without giving you these," she said nervously, pointing to a basket of biscuits with a jar of her homemade honey and jam mixture.

"You didn't have to do this," Jessie replied.

"I know," Ellie murmured, looking her in the eyes.

Jessie sighed, breaking the stare as she looked down at the basket.

Ellie closed the distance between them, pressing her lips to Jessie's. The simple kiss ended as quickly as it had begun, but it took Ellie's body an extra second to realize it was over. Every hair on her body stood up as if she were electrically charged. Her chest heaved liked she'd just outrun a horse. The sensation of kissing another woman had been like nothing she'd ever felt before.

"What was that for?" Jessie whispered.

"Now, you don't have to think about it anymore," Ellie replied.

"Think about what?"

"What it's like to kiss me." She smiled.

Jessie grinned and shook her head.

"You should get going. Bert's probably pacing next to the wagon."

"He keeps telling me to bring you flowers."

Ellie folded her arms and laughed. "He's a smart man."

"How would that look? Me bringing you flowers?"

"Well, I just kissed you, so...I guess about the same." Ellie shrugged. "I've never kissed anyone I didn't intend to marry," she uttered, thinking out loud. "Certainly, never another woman."

"What's that supposed to mean?"

"I...I don't know..." She rubbed her temple. "You should go, Marshal. You have work to do."

Feeling like Ellie might be regretting what she'd done, Jessie grabbed the basket and left the store so she didn't have to hear her say it. When she walked outside, Bert was leaning against the wagon with his feet crossed at the ankles, and his hands on his gun belt. The sun was just starting to change the color of the sky in the distance behind Boone Mountain.

Jessie climbed up and set the basket on the wagon seat, then she hopped back down. "Come on, let's get moving," she mumbled, walking inside the office.

***

The wagon moved at a good pace, leaving the Boone Creek town limit quickly and heading across the prairie. The sun was moving higher and higher, nearly clearing the mountains as it colored the sky in hues of orange and red. Jessie held the reins, giving gentle tugs left and right to keep them on the path as the wagon bounced along. The trail was a little more than wide enough for two wagons to pass, and full of rocks and divots. Bert sat beside her as the lookout, scanning his eyes in all directions, while their prisoner, Shamus Maguire, was handcuffed to the bench he was sitting on in the back.

"Open that basket," Jessie said.

"What is it?" Bert asked.

"Biscuits."

"Ms. Ellie made you biscuits?"

"No. She made *us* biscuits."

"She likes you, you know," he said, opening the lid. "Oh, these smell good."

Jessie took a biscuit and dipped it in the jar of honey jam, while holding the reins in one hand. "They taste even better," she said, taking a big bite. "What makes you think she likes me?" she asked, chewing her food.

"This is the second time she's made you biscuits, plus she's made you tea. I assume you'll be getting married soon."

Jessie began coughing as she choked on the food she'd swallowed. Bert handed her his cup of coffee, which she gulped down. At the same time, Shamus laughed hysterically in the back of the wagon.

"Shut up before I shoot you," Jessie growled, looking back at him. Her eyes grew large when she saw something in the distance. "Son of a bitch!" she yelled.

"Get that shotgun, Bert!" She slapped the reins on the horses' backsides, making them run faster.

Four masked men on horseback were coming up fast behind them, two on each side.

"Come on, boys!" Shamus cheered.

The men began shooting at them as they got closer.

"Shoot, Bert! Damn it!" she shouted, slapping the reins over and over. "Come on, you old mules!"

Bert fired a shot, but they were too far away for the shotgun pellets to reach them. He reloaded as the wagon bounced all around, nearly throwing him off the side. Jessie drew her pistol and turned sideways in the seat. She held the reins in one hand and fired her gun with the other as one of them tried to come up alongside the wagon. Her bullet hit him in the chest, causing the man to fall back off the horse.

Gunfire rang back and forth as Jessie and Bert fought off the other three men. The wagon hit a rock, lurching it to the side. Bert tumbled out and his coat hung up on the seat. Being dragged alongside the wagon, he held on for dear life.

"Hold on!" Jessie yelled. She tied the reins to the seat, then slid over. "Give me your hand!"

Bert reached back as far as he could. Jessie grabbed his hand, then reached around his body with the other hand to try and pull him up. Two bullets ricocheted and busted through the side of the wooden wagon rail, narrowly missing Shamus.

"Shoot them, not me. You fool!" he shouted. The splintered side was near where he was shackled. He began smashing his arm into the splintered wood, trying to bust the eyelet free.

Jessie planted her feet and tugged as hard as she could, finally pulling Bert back up into the seat as the wagon raced out of control. Bert reached for the shotgun slapping up and down on the floor. Jessie saw another one of the men trying to come alongside. She shot him in the chest. Then, she reloaded her pistol, and grabbed the other gun from her belt. With a gun in each hand, she fired over and over.

Bert got the shotgun loaded and fired at the closest horseman, blowing a hole right threw him, just as Shamus finally broke free. He leapt forward, trying to get the gun from Bert. The last masked man came up on the other side, where Jessie had her back to him. She tucked the extra gun into her belt and held onto her pistol while she helped Bert fight off Shamus.

Suddenly, the wagon hit a large rock and leapt high in the air on one side. The jolt knocked Bert sideways and he let go of the gun. Shamus fell back with it in his hands. Before he could turn it around and get a shot off, Jessie squeezed the trigger of her Peacemaker. The bullet passed through his forehead above his right eye. Another shot rang out next to her ear, causing her hearing to buzz. She saw the fourth guy's body bounce on the ground where he'd fallen from the side of the wagon. Turning her head, she saw Bert staring wide-eyed with his pistol in his hand.

"Whoa!!" Jessie yelled, trying to stop the horses after she untied the reins.

They dug their hooves in and she pulled the brake. They bounced around before coming to a halt. Jessie and Bert stared at each other in disbelief. Shamus was dead in the back of the wagon, and the other four members of his gang were lying dead along about a two mile path.

"What the hell just happened?" Bert muttered, trying to catch his breath and slow his racing heart.

"We got ambushed. How in the hell did they know when we'd be transporting him?" Jessie snapped, shaking her head.

"I don't know," he said.

"Fuck!" she yelled.

"What are we going to do?"

"We have to round up the bodies and head back to Boone Creek. We'll send a telegram to the justice, explaining what happened," she sighed. "I knew I should've shot you in the theatre," she mumbled, looking at Shamus's dead body.

SIXTEEN

It took Jessie and Bert over an hour to round up the other four bodies as they headed back up the path towards Boone Creek. The horses were moving much slower after racing at full speed for such a long distance, and the wagon wheels had become wobbly from the wild ride. By the time they'd found the last guy, the sun was high in the cloudless sky, and beating down on them. They were sweaty and exhausted. Bert was covered in dirt from being drug alongside the wagon, and Jessie had trail dust on her from it being kicked up by the horses. Somehow, they'd lost both Ellie's basket and the stage gun, which they'd found not too far from the fourth guy. The basket, however, was nowhere in sight.

***

When the wagon rolled into town full of bullet holes, splatters of blood, and five dead bodies, several town folk gasped in horror. Jessie guided the horses over to Doc Vernon's office and yelled, "Whoa!" They came to a stop and she pulled the brake. After tying the reins to the footboard, she climbed down. "Go get the mayor," she said to the nearest guy. He quickly took off running.

"What in the world?" Doc Vernon mumbled, walking outside. "Are you two all right?"

"We are," Bert said, "but they're not." He nodded over his shoulder towards the back of the wagon.

Doc Vernon peered over the side at the five dead men. "Oh, my word!"

Mayor Montgomery's horse raced down the center of Main Street, skidding to a stop nearby. He jumped down, handing the reins to a bystander to tie up. "Jessie?" he questioned, looking at the two disheveled law officers. "What happened?"

"We got ambushed about an hour outside of town," she answered. "We managed to stop three of them. Then, Shamus got loose. He and the fourth guy put up a huge fight. Bert fell out of the wagon and was drug a few hundred yards."

"You two are lucky to be alive," he said, shaking his head. "Neither of you got shot?" he asked, looking at all of the holes in the wagon.

"No," they said simultaneously.

Most of the town folk had made their way down to the end of town. Some came to see the bodies of the Dirty Boys Gang, others came to see if Bert and Jessie were okay. Molly raced through the crowd, searching for Bert.

"I'm okay, Molly," he said. "I just went for a wild ride, is all."

"My God, you look like you got dragged by a horse."

"Well..." He looked at Jessie and shook his head. "Things got a bit hairy for a minute, but we pulled through."

"Are you all right?" Lita asked, putting her hand on Jessie's back. "I came as soon as I heard."

"I'm fine," Jessie said, turning around.

Lita wrapped her arms around Jessie, causing everyone around them to gasp in shock. At the same time,

Jessie's eyes caught sight of Ellie in the crowd. Their eyes met and Ellie shook her head, before spinning around and walking away.

"Ellie!" Jessie called. "Ellie, wait!" She politely pushed Lita off of her and to the side. "Excuse me. Pardon me," she said over and over as she made her way to the edge of the gathering. "Ellie, please wait," she pleaded.

"It looks like you have plenty of comfort," Ellie said. She'd stopped and spun around. "It's fine. I just…I only wanted to make sure you were okay…is all. I'm glad you weren't hurt," Ellie stammered, taking a deep breath. "The last thing this town needs is to lose another marshal," she added. "I'm glad Bert's okay, too."

"You know I don't want her," Jessie replied, stepping closer.

***

Pastor Noah had made his way down to see what all of the commotion was about. The crowd's focus had shifted from the wagon full of dead men, to the two women having an intimate conversation. He had the same raised eyebrow look as everyone else as they all listened closely.

***

"Your personal life is none of my business," Ellie said.

"Damn it, Ellie. What if I want it to be?"

"Huh?" Ellie mumbled, unsure what to say.

"I could've died out there today, and all I could think about was you. I've never been like this with anyone in my life." Jessie shook her head. "I don't know how to be proper, and I know I'm not a man, but I've seen it your eyes. I know you feel it, too."

Ellie stared at her, unable to speak.

"Marry me, Ellie Fray."

"What?" she squeaked, inhaling sharply. "Why on earth would I do that?"

"So I can kiss you properly and tell you how much I love you," Jessie said, dropping to one knee and grabbing Ellie's hand. "Tell me you don't feel the same, and I'll walk away. I'll even leave town, if you want me to."

A tear rolled down Ellie's cheek. She put her hand to her mouth to cover her sob. Seeing the pleading green eyes staring back at her, Ellie couldn't help herself. She dropped to her knees, wrapping Jessie in a tight embrace. Jessie closed her eyes, inhaling the scent of Ellie's shampoo as she put her arms around Ellie and pressed her face against the side of her head.

Mayor Montgomery cleared his throat loudly. Jessie stood up, pulling Ellie to her feet at the same time. She turned to see the town folk had their eyes glued to them, and swallowed the lump in her throat as she glanced back at Ellie.

"Is that a yes?" she muttered.

"Jessie." Ellie smiled, liking the way if felt to say her name. "I...I don't know. Can we even do that? Get married?"

"I love you," Jessie said.

"I love you, too," Ellie whispered. "I really want to kiss you again," she murmured, almost inaudibly.

116

Pastor Noah moved closer. "It's none of my business, but God doesn't care, as long as you love each other. Mayor Montgomery, you know the laws better than I do."

The mayor chewed his mustache in thought. "I...um...I don't think there's anything, you know in the books." He shrugged. "Hell," he mumbled. "Pardon me, Pastor."

Pastor Noah smiled and nodded.

"If God says it's okay, then why not?" the mayor said.

Jessie grinned at Ellie. "Well?"

"Yes. Absolutely, yes." Ellie smiled brightly and wrapped Jessie in a hug.

"Do you think we could get this other matter cleared up, first, though?" The mayor questioned, tipping his hat towards the wagon.

"Oh...right." Jessie laughed.

"I need to get back to my store, anyhow. I'm so glad you're okay," Ellie added, stepping away from Jessie.

"The show is over folks. This is a law matter. Please go on home and give us some space to work," the mayor addressed the crowd. "Well, that went...way off course," he chuckled, removing his hat to wipe the sweat from his brow.

"No kidding," Jessie replied. "What are we going to do about these five?" she asked, looking in the back of the wagon.

"Let's let the undertaker handle them. You and Bert come on over to my office so we can get your statements together. Then, I'll wire the justice in Red Rock and let him know what happened. You two were obviously attacked and are lucky to be alive."

"That's because Marshal Henry can shoot a trade dollar out of the sky with her eyes closed," Bert said. "She's tried to teach me, but—"

"It looks like you did all right. You came back alive," Mayor Montgomery said as he climbed up on his horse.

"He did just fine, Mayor," Jessie called before he rode off.

"I'm only alive because you saved me. If you hadn't pulled me back in, I would've surely been run over by the wagon, or shot, or both," Bert said to her.

"Be my best man at my wedding, and we'll call it even."

"Uh…me? Really?"

"Well, who else?"

Bert smiled. "I'd be honored."

"Good, that's settled."

"I still think you should get her some flowers," Bert mumbled as they started walking towards the mayor's office.

Jessie shook her head and laughed.

SEVENTEEN

It had been a week since the ambush. Mayor Montgomery had sent a telegram to the justice in Red Rock, regarding the incident, to which he hadn't received a reply. The Dirty Boys Gang members were buried in Boot Hill in a funeral that no one attended except the undertaker, and his grave diggers. Things had somewhat slowed down around town, at least as far as crime was concerned. However, the weasel, Nicolas Munroe was still around.

"There hasn't been a drunken fight in several days," Bert said, thinking out loud as he watched the rain pour down outside of the Marshal's Office.

Jessie nodded and sipped her coffee. She loved the sound of the rain on the tin roof, especially when she didn't have to be out in it, getting soaking wet. "A day like today isn't going to help keep things calm, I'm afraid."

"Why is that?" he asked, sticking his head outside as a young messenger ran by, obviously coming from the post with a telegram.

Jessie ignored the passerby as she cleaned and oiled her pistol, something she did weekly to keep it in good condition. "Everyone's cooped up inside. When this storm lifts, they'll be twice as eager to gamble, get drunk, and find company."

Bert pursed his lips, thinking she was probably right. "It sure is quiet around here with Shamus gone," he mumbled, coming back inside.

"Are you bored, Bert?" Jessie asked, putting her oiling cloth away and re-holstering her gun.

"Well...no."

Jessie pulled a cigar from her pocket and struck a match against the wall beside her. "Sounds to me like you are," she replied, lighting her smoke.

"Marshal Henry!" the teenager yelled, splashing through the mud as he ran.

Jessie got up and walked to the open doorway. "Slow down, kid. What's going on?"

"Mayor Montgomery told me to come get you. He has a message from Red Rock," he panted.

Jessie nodded and handed him a dime. "Looks like I'm getting wet," she said to Bert as she extinguished her cigar, and pulled a rain slicker on over her coat. Large rain drops pelted down, soaking her hat and slicker as she rushed across the street, careful to avoid the puddles.

"You're going to catch a cold running around out there," Ellie said with a smile.

"I'll be all right. I have you to take care of me," Jessie replied from the doorway. She knew better than to go inside, dripping water all over the wooden floor of the store.

"Is that so?"

"You did say you would marry me, unless my ears hearing is failing me." Jessie grinned.

Ellie laughed. "Where are you off to in this mess?"

"I've been summoned by the mayor. He got a wire from Red Rock, probably something to do with the ambush."

"Do you think it's improper for me to invite you for supper?" Ellie asked, biting her lower lip.

Jessie shrugged. "I sort of threw proper out the window a long time ago."

"That's for sure. Still, I don't want the town folk to—"

"To what? Think you're not proper? Think you're being inappropriate? Ellie, you're marrying another woman. I'd hope you'd stopped caring what the people around here thought of you, at least by now."

"My business is my livelihood. Without it, I have nothing."

"If it's bothering you this much, then we can wait. Once we're married, we'll have supper together every night...in our home."

"That'll be nice. I'm not very fond of you boarding in that...that place," she grimaced.

"Then, set our wedding date. You tell me the day and the time, and I'll be there."

"How about tomorrow at noon?" Ellie blurted.

"Okay, then."

"Are you serious?" Ellie asked nervously.

"If tomorrow at noon works for you, then it works for me."

"You don't want to discuss it first?"

"Discuss what? You love me, right?"

"Yes, of course," Ellie huffed. "Don't be silly."

"I love you, too, and I want nothing more than to pull you into my arms and kiss you properly. I can't do that until we're married."

Ellie felt a blush creep up her cheeks. She pulled her eyes away from Jessie's before they gave away more than she'd wanted them to. "That'll be fine," she mumbled.

"Wonderful. Bert and I will see you at noon."

"Bert?"

"Yes. I've asked him to accompany me as my best man."

"I..." Ellie stammered. "I haven't chosen a maid of honor or a dress. Maybe tomorrow is too soon."

"You could wear a potato sack and I'd still think you were the most beautiful girl in town."

"Well, I can assure you, I will not be getting married in a sack." Ellie shook her head, trying to keep from laughing. "I don't know about closing the store in the middle of the day. It's only been closed one other time," she added.

"Is there something else going on?" Jessie grabbed her hand. "You're the one who said tomorrow at noon. If you need more time—"

"I did say that. You're right. I guess tomorrow is as good as any other day."

"Okay, then. Tomorrow at noon."

"Is the church available?"

"About the church...I was thinking maybe something outside."

"What do you mean? Outside of the church? Is that even allowed?" she questioned.

"I'm sure it is. I'll speak with Pastor Noah. I need to get going, the mayor is waiting."

"Be careful in that mud. Miss Mable will have a field day trying to get it out of your clothes."

"Miss Mable doesn't do my laundry."

"So, the harlot does that, too?" Ellie growled, crossing her arms in haste.

Jessie laughed. "What is it with you and Lita? I'm not sweet on her. In fact, I have never been in her company, other than at the saloon. She's merely a friend, and no, she doesn't do my laundry, either. If you must know…Ike does it."

"Ike? Since when does he wash clothes?"

"He washes mine twice a month. I pay him of course."

Ellie stared oddly at her.

"You're beautiful when you're mad. I noticed that the first day I met you."

"I'm not mad, and I wasn't then, by the way."

"Okay." Jessie grinned and tipped her hat before stepping back into the rain.

"Jessie Henry, you make me crazy," she called.

"Good. I feel the same," Jessie yelled with a big grin on her face.

***

Mayor Montgomery stood by the window, smoking a cigar. His hat and coat were on the rack nearby. He'd handed Jessie the telegram when she'd walked in.

She read over it…twice.

Mayor Montgomery,

Expect my presence in Boone Creek, one week from the 12th. I'll be conducting an inquiry into the events of the 5th, during which time Shamus Maguire was being transported to Red Rock to stand trial for murder. I will be holding interviews with Marshal Jessie Henry and Deputy Marshal Bert Boleyn in accordance with Law 18.2.34. Your presence is not required, but you are permitted to attend any and all meetings if you deem it necessary.

Regards,
Colorado Territory Justice Walker T. Samuelson

"Surely we're not being held responsible for an ambush that nearly killed the both of us," Jessie said, placing the paper onto his desk.

"No. That's not what the law states. He's merely coming here to finalize everything and close the case on Shamus Maguire. The two of you will give sworn statements about what happened, separately of course, then he'll write up a report and be on his way. He's an old friend, so I'm sure that's why he's coming here, rather than having you two go to him."

"I'll let Bert know."

"Any word on your wedding date?" he asked.

"Ms. Ellie said tomorrow at noon."

"That's pretty soon." He left the window and walked back to his desk. "There are mixed feelings around town, you know."

"I'm sure there are, but I don't get into anyone's business…so I'd hope they'd do me the same respect and not get into mine. Ms. Ellie is a business owner in this town. She's respected and well-liked. Shaming her for who she loves is…well it's nonsense."

"I never said anything was wrong with it. As long as you are happy and love each other, who am I to judge? Besides, Pastor Noah preaches the word of God, so if he agreed to marry you two, then it must be okay with him, as well."

Jessie nodded.

"Everything has to have a first one, and you've brought a lot of firsts to Boone Creek. The town folk have come to like you. Hell, you keep going, you're liable to be in my shoes one day."

She shook her head. "Politics is most definitely not for me."

"Never say never," Mayor Montgomery laughed.

"Looks like the rain is letting up," she said, seeing the sun in the distance.

"I hope so, or we'll be covered in mud for weeks."

***

Jessie took a detour back to the Marshal's Office since the weather had cleared, stopping at the Rustler's Den.

"It's about to get busy in here," she said, sitting on a stool.

"Yeah, rains always good for business. People hate to be cooped up. They don't have a whole lot to do with the theatre still being closed. You think it'll ever reopen?" Elmer asked, pouring a hot cup of coffee for her.

"Not as long as that weasel, Mr. Munroe, is in town pretending to buy it," she replied.

Elmer wiped the bar top with the towel he always had over his shoulder, then he placed the mug in front of her.

"You ever been married, Elmer?"

"Once," he muttered. "Long time ago. The fever took her."

"I'm sorry."

"Oh, don't be. I was just a kid."

"You never found anyone else?"

"No. Never really looked, either."

She drank her coffee and sighed. "Does it bother you?"

"What? You and Ms. Ellie getting married?"

Jessie nodded.

"Would it matter to you if it did?"

"No," she said.

"Then, why ask?"

"Just checking."

"Marshal Henry, I consider you a friend. So…no, it doesn't bother me."

"Good to know," she replied, digging into her vest pocket.

"Coffee's on the house." He smiled, waving her off as she tried to pay.

She slid off the stool and headed out the door, happy to see the sun in the sky. The rain had left massive puddles in its wake, which were impossible to step over.

"Well, if it isn't our town marshal," Otis muttered.

Jessie looked around, seeing the town drunk leaning against a hitching post outside of the stage office.

"You headed somewhere, Otis?"

"Nope, but you are," he called.

"And, where might that be?"

"To jail. I hear the territory justice is coming for you himself."

Jessie laughed. "What makes you think I'm going to jail?"

"There were no witnesses to that ambush…except the dead ones. It's mighty hard for them to defend themselves, don't you think?"

"What do you know about the law, you old bag of bones?" She shook her head and began walking. "Didn't I tell you to take a damn bath? You stink, Otis!" she called over her shoulder.

EIGHTEEN

Bert looked like the cat that ate the canary when Jessie walked into the Marshal's Office. She raised a brow and waited. It took all of ten seconds before he blurted out everything.

"Molly is helping Ms. Ellie with the wedding. She came over after you left and asked me what I thought about her asking Molly to be her matron of honor. I told her I thought she'd be delighted. Turns out, she was. Molly's been over there for the past hour."

Jessie shook her head and laughed. "Bert, you sound like a damn puppet. What Ms. Ellie does before the wedding isn't any of my concern. I'm glad your Molly is assisting her. However, I have other things to contend with...like Justice Samuelson coming to town next week to conduct an inquiry on the ambush."

"Are you serious? What for?"

"He has to interview us and get all of the facts so the territory can close the case on Shamus Maguire." She watched him fidget for a second. "Don't worry, all we have to do is tell him the truth. They came up on us, guns-a-blazing. We fought back, and we happened to be better shots. It's as simple as that. Now, where are these flowers you keep telling me to get?"

Bert grinned. "Near the edge of the town limit. There are fields of purple, pink, and blue flowers growing

Graysen Morgen

everywhere. Get a couple handfuls, tie them up with a silk ribbon, and there you go."

"Great. I have a few more things to do, so I'll meet you tonight for rounds in Six Gun Alley," she said, leaving once again. She glanced over at the General Trade, before turning the curve and carrying on at a brisk pace.

***

"Hello?" Jessie called from outside the doorway of the church. "Anyone here?"

"Well...I wondered when I'd see you," Pastor Noah said, walking up behind her.

Jessie jumped, nearly drawing her gun on him.

"Whoa, now! Don't shoot. I'm unarmed," he kidded.

"Sneaking up on a marshal probably isn't a good idea," she stated.

"You're right. My apologies. Although, in fairness, I didn't intend to startle you. I saw you walk over, and I was headed back here anyhow. I just happened to be behind you."

"I came to ask a favor of you."

"So, I've heard. You and Ms. Ellie plan to marry tomorrow. Is that correct?"

"Yes, but if you're not available with it being short notice and all—"

"No," he paused for a second. "No. Aside from a little work I have to do on my sermon for Sunday, my schedule is pretty clear."

"Great. We plan to marry at noon. Is that all right?"

"Marshal, God doesn't care what time you get married, and frankly, I don't either. Noon is fine with me.

That doesn't give you much time to get over that phobia of yours though."

"What phobia?"

"Well, stepping inside my church, of course."

"Oh...no. That's not happening. I'd like to do it outside, under a tree maybe."

"You want to get married...under a tree?"

"Sure. Why not?"

Pastor Noah raised a brow. "That's not exactly...tradition."

"Two women are getting married...to each other. I'm pretty sure that's not traditional, either."

"You're right." He thought for a second. "The word of God is the word of God. It doesn't really matter where it's received, I suppose. Traditionally, it's in a church, but not always, I guess." He looked at Jessie. "I'll make a deal with you. You know Ms. Ellie comes to service every Sunday. If you make it a point to come with her one Sunday a month, I'll perform your service under whatever tree you choose."

Jessie bit her lower lip. Church was the absolute last place she ever wanted to be. "Will it suffice if I sit outside the door and listen?"

"If that is the closest that I'm going to get you to stepping inside this building, then...we have a deal."

"One Sunday a month, and I can listen from out here," she said, pointing to where she was standing, a few feet from the church entrance.

He nodded and said, "I'll leave a chair for you."

"Deal."

"Good," he replied. "Although, I hope one day you see that it's okay to come inside. God doesn't judge the living, he condemns the dead. Our souls pay for the sins of our bodies long after we've served our time in this world. Remember that."

"I will," she replied.

"All right, now that we have that squared away, where is this tree you speak of?"

"I haven't found it yet."

"What? You talk me into holding your ceremony outside of the sanctity of the church, and you don't even have a location?" Pastor Noah shook his head and laughed. "I suggest you go find a tree, Marshal. You're running out of time."

"More like daylight," she muttered, looking at the position of the sun.

"What time are we meeting at this unknown tree?"

"Noon," she said. "I'll find you in the morning and let you know where to go. I still have a few more things to do. Thank you again for doing this."

"Oh, no thanks needed." He grinned.

Jessie headed back past the General Trade and Pearl Hall. She sighed as she glanced at the *Closed* sign, and kept walking. The Fashionette sat just on the other side. Ike was finishing with a customer when she walked in.

"Marshal, what can I do for you?" he asked.

"I'm getting married tomorrow."

"I heard something about that from Ms. Nelly over at the Kettle Kitchen. Congratulations."

"Thanks. I need..." Jessie looked around.

"Something other than black, I suppose?" he asked with a smirk.

"No," she retorted. "Something newer."

"You can't get married in that funeral outfit you wear."

"Funeral? What's wrong with my clothes? I'm a law officer. Black is traditional."

Ike bit back a laugh. "Marshal Henry, you are anything but traditional."

"Fine. What color do you suggest?" she scowled.

"Let me go to the back and see what I have that will fit you."

Jessie walked around, looking at various items as she waited. The bell above the door jingled as another patron stepped inside. She turned to see Nicolas. "Mr. Munroe," she said, tipping her hat.

"Marshal Henry." He nodded. "I hear you have big plans for tomorrow," he said sarcastically.

"That is correct."

"I would say I wish you well, but…Oh, hell. Why not?" He shrugged. "Best of luck to you."

"Did you need to see Ike?" she asked as he began to leave.

"I can come back another time. He's busy getting you ready for your big day. I wouldn't want to impose, you know, steal him away from you or anything." He gave a fake grin and walked out the door.

"Was someone here?" Ike asked, coming from the back with a single vest.

"Yeah, Mr. Munroe," she said, still staring at the door.

"Hmm." He shrugged. "All right, so I have a blue vest with a paisley pattern. The rest of my stock is too large. A black puff tie or a narrow neck tie like the one you're wearing now will go well with it. Or, I have both types of ties in several colors, if you want to stay with your black vest.

Jessie looked at each one. She knew nothing about clothes and colors. "I don't know, Ike. What do you think?"

"Try each one on and go from there," he said. "Personally, I like the black tie and colored vest combo, but you're not one for that much color, so I'd go with the burgundy puff tie with your black vest."

"That'll work," she said, pulling a coin from her vest pocket to pay for the new tie.

***

When Jessie had finally called it a night, she headed to Miss Mable's to get some sleep. Since she was getting married the next day, this would be her last night as a boarder in the brothel house, something Ellie was more than pleased about.

"I was wondering when I would see you," Lita said, from her position on the staircase. She was leaning against the wall with one leg hiked up on a higher step, spreading the front of her cinched dress and revealing the smooth skin of her upper thighs.

"It's been a long day," Jessie replied in passing.

Lita grabbed her arm. "Are you sure marrying that shopkeeper is really what you want?"

"Why is that any of your concern?"

Lita moved closer, running her hand up the front of Jessie's vest. "I can make you feel better than she can," she murmured, slowly closing the space between them.

"I'm sure you make a lot of people feel wonderful. In fact, I hear it just about every night. So, I'm well aware of what you can do," Jessie said, grabbing Lita's hand and moving it away from her chest. "However, you are not the person I am interested in spending the rest of my life with. You're a pretty woman, Lita, but I don't love you. I don't want your company. I never have, and I never will." Jessie continued up the stairs.

"You're making a mistake. She doesn't love you, she's just lonely," Lita spat.

"And you're pitiful. Get yourself together!" she sneered through gritted teeth.

NINETEEN

Jessie woke up around her usual time and packed her stuff. Everything she'd acquired in the six months that she'd been in town, fit neatly into a canvas sack. She set it to the side and got dressed, saving her new, burgundy puff-tie for last. She wasn't sure she liked the way it fit, but it did look nice when she glanced at the tiny mirror. Finishing off with her gun belt, coat, and hat, she headed out the door.

"Big day for you, Marshal," Miss Mable said with a smile. "That Ellie Fray is a lucky lady."

"I'm pretty sure, I'm the lucky one," Jessie replied. "I'll be back later this afternoon to retrieve my things."

"That'll be fine."

Bert walked around the corner, just as Jessie stepped outside.

"Well, would you look at that. Marshal Henry got herself a new tie."

"Do you want to eat this tie, Bert?" Jessie asked.

"Huh?"

She shook her head. "Come on, we have to find a tree."

"What for?" he questioned, falling in step next to her.

Jessie ignored him as they walked around to where the stable and corral were located, along with the livery. "We need a pair of horses for the hour, and a couple of long ropes," she said. "Marshal business. Put it on the mayor's bill."

"Yes, ma'am," the young stable-hand replied. He quickly saddled up two mares and grabbed a pair of lassos.

Jessie tipped him a couple of small coins for his speedy service, and climbed up on the horse, looping the rope around the saddle horn. Bert followed as she slapped the reins, trotting the large animal off towards Pinewood Pass. They cut off the main path and onto a cattle trail near the creek that flowed a steady stream of cool, mountain water.

"Whoa," Jessie said a few minutes later, pulling gently on the reins as the big oak came into view. She hopped down and looped the reins around one of the thick branches.

"This is where you taught me to shoot my pistol," Bert said, tying up his horse. "What are we doing out here?"

"This is where I'm getting married."

"What about the church?"

Jessie pinned him with a stare. "Have you ever seen me in the church?"

"No."

"Then what makes you think I'm going in there now?" She shook her head. "Churches and I don't mix."

"Well, it's definitely a pretty tree, even with all of my stray bullet holes."

"Let's move that old log over. I don't think anyone else will be here, but in case anyone shows, they'll have a place to sit."

Bert nodded and helped her tie the lassos to the horses' saddle horns. Then, they tied them to the tree trunk and used the horses to pull it into place.

"I think this will work just fine. How about you?" she said, standing back and taking a look.

"I think it's perfect."

"Good. When you get back, I need you to inform Ms. Ellie of the location, as well as anyone else who wishes to join us."

"Where are you going?"

"I have a few other things to do. I'll be around in time. Don't worry."

"All right," he said, climbing up into the saddle of his horse and riding off.

Jessie headed in the opposite direction, towards a large patch of wild flowers in the distance. She picked more than a handful of the colorful flowers and arranged them as best she could, before tying a satin ribbon around them. She crisscrossed it all the way down the stems and back up to make it more sturdy. Then, she took it over to the large tree and set it on a branch.

***

At ten minutes to noon, Jessie stood under the tree, with Bert next to her, holding the flowers. She watched as Pastor Noah made his way down the path with Ellie holding his arm, and the bible in his hands. Ellie looked very different from her every day clothing in a bright, purple skirt with a black floral pattern and black lace trim, and a white, high-collared blouse. The top button of her shirt was in the shape of a beautiful purple rose. Her light brown hair was braided, and then wrapped into a twist at the base of her head. A petite, purple hat with black lace trim, was pinned to the top of her head in the front.

"You look beautiful," Jessie said, handing Ellie the flowers as she took her place across from her.

"I like your tie. It brings out your eyes," Ellie replied, sniffing the flowers. "These smell wonderful."

Pastor Noah cleared his throat. "If I could have everyone's attention, there is a log down front here for those of you who wish to sit. We'll be getting started momentarily."

Jessie pulled her eyes away from Ellie and gasped. Elmer, Ike, Miss Mable, Ms. Nelly, Mayor Montgomery, and a handful of other town folk, were standing in front of them. "My word," she whispered. "They must all be here for you," she said to Ellie.

"I doubt it. You've made quite an impression on this town, Marshal Henry."

"After today, you can finally stop calling me marshal."

"I look forward to it."

"Shall we begin?" Pastor Noah said, stepping up to them with his bible held open.

Jessie felt her legs tremble. She forced them still and took a few calming, deep breaths as she looked at Ellie, who nodded in his direction.

"Today, these two people join hands in marriage in front of God, with all of you as witnesses," he began. "God says, love is like a seal over your heart, for it is as strong as death, and its jealousy unyielding as the grave. It burns like blazing fire with a mighty flame that many waters cannot quench and rivers cannot wash away. Jessie Henry, is this true of your love for Ellie Fray?"

"It is," she said.

"Ellie Fray, is this true of your love for Jessie Henry?"

"Yes," she replied.

"Do we have rings?" he asked.

Jessie nodded and retrieved two silver bands from her vest pocket. Pastor Noah placed them in the center of the open bible.

"These rings are but a symbol of your commitment to this marriage and to each other. As they become worn with age, let them forever be a testament to your undying love for one another," he stated. "Jessie, place the ring on Ellie's hand and repeat after me: Never will I leave you, nor forsake you."

Jessie did as she was told, albeit with shaky hands.

"Ellie, place the ring on Jessie's hand and repeat after me: Never will I leave you, nor forsake you."

She held her breath to calm her nerves, before repeating the words.

"Please join hands," he said. He put one of his hands over theirs. "Let us bow our heads. God, we stand before you today to unite Jessie and Ellie in holy matrimony. I ask for your blessing upon this ceremony and this marriage. I ask that the love they share at this moment, grows and matures with each passing year, filling their hearts with happiness, forgiveness, and faith. Amen." He closed the bible, keeping his hand on theirs. "Today, two become united as one. May no one ever split apart what God has joined together." He removed his hand and smiled. "By the word of God, I pronounce you married. You may kiss each other now."

Jessie leaned forward, pressing her lips softly to Ellie's in a sincere, but simple kiss that left her wanting more.

"I present to you Jessie and Ellie Henry," Pastor Noah said.

Everyone clapped, and Jessie and Bert drew their pistols, each firing a single shot in the air at the same time. After holstering her gun, Jessie grabbed Ellie's hand and together, they walked away.

"Where are we going?" Ellie asked, letting go of Jessie's hand and linking arms with her.

"Apparently, we've been invited to the Rustler's Den for a gathering in our favor."

Ellie nodded with a smile.

The people who had come to witness the ceremony, had tagged along behind the happy couple as they led the way back through town along the sidewalk. Otis muddled along in the street, ranting about the lady law, all of which Jessie ignored.

A loud noise grabbed their attention. Everyone looked up to see a runaway wagon with two horses, racing down the center of Main Street, out of control as the driver fought to climb out onto one of the horses to retrieve the broken reins. Jessie saw Otis, still mumbling away as it headed straight for him. Instinctively, she let go of Ellie and ran into the street, shoving him out of the way and diving to the ground as the wagon roared past, narrowly missing them. They lay on the ground, covered in dirt as the dust settled. The driver finally grabbed a piece of leather strap and was able to get the wagon stopped, much further down the street.

"Get off of me, Lady Law!" Otis growled.

Graysen Morgen

"She just saved your scrawny ass. The least you could do is thank her," the mayor spat.

Otis burped and hiccupped as he said an impolite thank you and wandered off.

Jessie shook her head as she brushed some of the dirt off her clothes. "So much for looking nice," she muttered.

Ellie smiled. "Trouble always has a way of finding you, doesn't it?"

"Something like that," Jessie replied with a grin.

***

"The first one's on the house," Elmer said to the group gathered around inside the saloon, as he began pouring thimble shots of whiskey.

Jessie took the first cup and climbed up onto a table with her drink raised in the air. As her best man, Bert grabbed the next, and so on until everyone had a thimble in their hand. "If you know me, you know I don't talk much," she said. "So, I'd just like to thank each of you for coming to our wedding. This was our special day, and we are happy to be sharing it with those whom we consider our friends." She smiled at Ellie and chugged her glass.

For the next hour, Percy, the pianist, played song after song as everyone danced, drank, and played a few hands of Faro and Dice. Everyone who had attended the ceremony under the tree, had joined them in the reception at the saloon. As the guests left, one by one to go back to their daily life, they each congratulated the couple and handed Jessie a coin of varying value. It was tradition, as

  Boone Creek

well as common courtesy, to give the new groom a monetary gift.

Once everyone had gone, Elmer opened the saloon back up to regular patrons. On their way out, Jessie handed him an eagle coin.

"I won't accept this," he said, giving it back.

"Elmer—"

"You go on, now." He shooed her away. "Take that beautiful bride of yours home."

"Okay, then," she said, grabbing Ellie's hand.

"Do you need to go get your things?" Ellie asked, nodding towards Six Gun Alley where the brothel was located.

"I'll get them later. It's not much," she replied, squeezing Ellie's hand as they began walking down the sidewalk towards the General Trade.

***

Jessie removed her hat and looked around the open room that Ellie called home. It was the same size as the store below. A kitchenette with a wood burning stove for cooking and heat, was along one wall, with a small, dining-style table and two chairs nearby. Another pair of chairs sat in the middle of the room on a large, round rug, with a small table between them. A double bed was along the far wall in the back, with night stands on both sides. A dressing curtain was close to the bed area, with a handmade clothing rack behind it, full of Ellie's clothes. A pair of shoes sat on the floor under it.

"It's not much, but—"

"It's home, and anywhere that you are, is home to me," Jessie said, pulling Ellie into her arms. Their lips met in a soft kiss. Jessie took Ellie's hands and placed them on her face before wrapping her arms around Ellie's waist, pulling their bodies fully together.

Ellie gasped against her lips. "I...I don't...know what to do," she whispered.

"I'll show you," Jessie murmured, deepening the kiss. The touch of Ellie's tongue against hers made Jessie weak in the knees.

Ellie couldn't help moving her hips against Jessie's as she wrapped her arms around her neck. She'd never wanted anything so badly in her life, yet she had no idea what it was that she'd wanted. She just knew she wanted it. Her chest burned with a yearning she'd never felt before.

Jessie moved her hands up Ellie's sides, over the edge of her breasts, to the top button of her blouse. She ended the kiss, looking into Ellie's brown eyes as she opened one button at a time. Ellie moved her shaky hands over Jessie's shoulders to the top of her chest. She'd never undressed anyone or had someone undress her.

Jessie let go of the blouse she was opening and removed her coat, tossing it aside. Then, she unclasped her tie, adding it to the pile. She placed her hands on her vest to remove it, and Ellie grabbed them, stopping her.

Ellie held her breath as she unbuttoned the vest and pushed it off Jessie's shoulders. It dropped to the floor behind them without a sound. Their eyes met again as they continued undressing each other, pausing here and there to share long, sensual kisses, until there was nothing left but their undergarments. Ellie had on traditional bloomers and a camisole. Jessie's bloomers were cut shorter, stopping at mid-thigh instead of just above the knee, and she'd worn nothing under her shirt, so she still had it on as well.

Ellie ran her eyes over the woman in front of her, from head to toe, then she reached up, unbuttoning Jessie's shirt. After the last button, she spread the garment open. Her breath hitched at the sight of Jessie's bare torso. Her breasts were small with beady, pink nipples.

Jessie grabbed Ellie's hands, placing them on her breasts. Then, she shrugged out of her shirt, leaving her nude from the waist up. Ellie's heart raced as she nervously ran her hands over Jessie's upper body from her breasts to her flat stomach and back up again. Jessie put her hand under Ellie's chin, lifting it slightly.

Ellie's eye traced a path from her breasts up to the green eyes gazing back at her. She licked her lips and pressed them to Jessie's, kissing her with as much ardor as she could while relishing in the soft skin under her finger tips.

Jessie reached down, grasping the edge of Ellie's camisole on both sides of her waist and tugging it up. Ellie pulled her hands from Jessie's body long enough to have the camisole lifted away, revealing bouncy breasts that were bigger than Jessie's but not over-sized for her petite frame. Jessie bit her lower lip as her eyes took in the sight in front of her, and her hands ran gently over Ellie's creamy-colored, silky, smooth skin. She'd never wanted someone so badly.

Ellie's knees wobbled weakly with Jessie's caress. She nearly fell into Jessie's arms as their bodies came together. The feeling of another woman pressed against her made Ellie's body betray her. She rocked against Jessie as warm, wetness seeped into her bloomers.

Jessie's mouth met Ellie's in a deep, desirable kiss that left them both panting. She removed her own bloomers, tossing them to the side as Ellie did the same. "You're so beautiful, Ellie," she murmured.

Ellie smiled shyly. 'I've never...'" she muttered, swallowing the lump in her throat. "I've never been naked with anyone, before," she finished shakily as her body trembled, more from the yearning deep inside, than nervousness.

"But, you were married," Jessie said, grabbing her hand. "Weren't you intimate?"

"Yes, of course...but, not like this." She waved her free hand between the two of them.

Jessie nodded and pulled Ellie into her arms once more, bringing their full bodies together. She leaned back slightly, meeting Ellie's gaze, before kissing her tenderly.

Ellie deepened this kiss, searching for Jessie's tongue as Jessie's leg slipped between hers.

"Oh, my..." she gasped.

Jessie smiled, feeling the wetness coat her thigh. She ran her hands up and down Ellie's back while slowly moving her leg. Ellie shivered in her arms as her legs spread further. Jessie kissed the delicate skin of her shoulder and neck, up under her ear, and pulled the pins from her hair, allow it to fall freely and hang down her back in natural, loose waves.

Ellie moaned in protest as Jessie pulled away. She grabbed Jessie's hand and allowed her to lead them to the bed. She watched as Jessie pulled back the quilt. Then, she climbed onto the bed, lying on her side. Mimicking her position, Jessie pressed their lips together once more. She ran her hand over Ellie's body, before rolling her to her back, and moving on top of her.

Boone Creek

Ellie ran her hands up and down Jessie's back, reveling in the feeling of her smooth skin as they continued to trade kisses, until Jessie pulled away. Sliding her body down until her face was even with Ellie's breasts, Jessie placed delicate kisses across her chest, careful to avoid the perky, pink nipples. Unsure of what to do, Ellie simply let herself enjoy the tender touches as she watched Jessie move her mouth side to side. She gasped and hissed when Jessie sucked a nipple between her lips, teasing it with her tongue before releasing it.

Jessie looked up and smiled at the brown eyes staring at her. She kept her pace excruciatingly slow as she ran her tongue around the outside of the other nipple, then fully over it. Ellie released a panting sound that she'd never heard before, causing her to look away in embarrassment.

Jessie paused and moved back up to see her eyes. "Are you okay?" she asked.

Ellie nodded, then bit her lower lip. "What are you doing to me?" she whispered.

"I'll stop if you want me to," Jessie said, pulling back to look at her.

"No...No, don't stop," Ellie replied softly, running her hand through Jessie's hair.

Jessie smiled and met her lips once more as her hand moved along Ellie's body. Her palm slid down the side of her torso to her hip, then all the way back up at an agonizing pace, over and over, teasing her fingers lower with each pass. Ellie was nearly breathless by the time Jessie's fingers slipped between her legs, lazily stroking up and down. Her hips rose as high as they could with Jessie lying halfway on top of her.

146

"Oh!" Ellie cried out.

Jessie kissed the soft skin on the side of Ellie's neck, before moving her head down to suckle her breasts. Ellie's body jerked around under her as she applied more pressure with her fingers, then pushed two of them inside of her.

"I've got you," Jessie whispered as Ellie's body began to tremble.

"What...oh...oh my..." Ellie panted breathlessly.

Jessie touched her thumb to Ellie's center with each thrust until Ellie tightened around her fingers. Jessie stilled her hand and simply held Ellie as the wave of pleasure rolled through her.

Ellie's body went limp and collapsed under her, causing Jessie to grin as she rolled to Ellie's side. With her free hand, she wiped away the sweat on Ellie's brow, then she kissed her softly.

"My God," Ellie puffed, sounding a little winded. "What...was that?"

"That's called making love," Jessie replied, still smiling at her.

"I've certainly never felt anything like that before...not with anyone."

"Maybe that's because you were meant to be with me," Jessie teased, kissing her again.

Ellie ran her hand over Jessie's cheek. "I love the way your skin feels. It's so soft."

"I love you," Jessie said, turning her head and kissing her palm.

"Show me how make love to you," Ellie murmured, staring into her green eyes.

Jessie rolled to her back, pulling Ellie up against her side in the process. Then, grabbing her hand, she placed it on her breast and pushed it lower, down across her stomach to the top of her thigh. Spreading her legs, she ran Ellie's hand between them, pushing her fingers into the wetness at her center. Jessie's hips bucked as she showed her how to move in delicate circles, applying just the right amount of pressure. Moving her hand away, Jessie let Ellie take control.

"It's okay," Jessie encouraged. "You'll feel it when you're doing it right."

Ellie nodded nervously.

Jessie pulled her down into a searing kiss. Losing her train of thought, Ellie began moving her fingers in a slow, enticing rhythm.

Jessie fought to keep a steady breath and slow her building climax. It had been so long since she'd been touched, she'd forgotten how good it felt. Sensing Ellie dip down lower, she grabbed her hand, pushing her inside, then, showed her how to work her fingers in and out. She threw her head back, moaning when Ellie took over, her timidness obviously gone as she stroked her with ease.

"Mmmm," Jessie growled, stilling Ellie's hand as the euphoria washed over her. Completely spent, she pulled Ellie's hand free and wrapped her in a hug.

Ellie pressed her lips to Jessie's. "That was the most powerful thing I've ever experienced," she murmured, kissing her again. "I love you, Jessie Henry."

"I love you, too," Jessie whispered as her heart rate gradually found its way back to normal.

"I look forward to making love again," Ellie said quietly.

Jessie rolled Ellie to her back and moved over her. "How about right now?" she grinned, kissing her passionately.

TWENTY

"Good morning," Jessie said, coming down the metal, spiral staircase with a cup of coffee in one hand and her hat in the other.

Ellie looked up and smiled. "I was wondering when you'd appear," she replied, glancing at the clock.

Jessie walked over, setting her mug and hat down on the counter, before pulling Ellie into her arms. "I know I won't get to wake up next to you every day, because we keep different hours, but you're still the first thing I see before I start my day," she murmured, kissing her softly.

"Waking up next to you *is* quite nice," Ellie said. "So is going to bed beside you," she blushed.

Jessie grinned. "I should probably get going. Justice Samuelson will be here in a week, so I'm sure the mayor will be on edge with daily meetings."

"I thought all of that was over…"

"So did we, but he's coming to personally interview Bert and I about the ambush."

"Surely, he doesn't think you're fibbing."

"I doubt that. He's a smart man. I'm sure everything is fine. He and the mayor are old friends, so it's probably more of a social call," Jessie said, not wanting to alarm her new bride. "I'm not sure what time I'll be home, but I'll be here for supper before I go walk the alley tonight."

"I know. I'll see you when I see you. Not much has changed," Ellie said. "You have a town to watch over, and I have a store to run."

"Everything has changed...at least for me it has," Jessie replied, grabbing her hand.

"I didn't mean it in a bad way. I always looked forward to the possibility of seeing you during the day. Now that we're married, I don't have to wonder if I'll see you in the street, or if you'll pop in to buy something, because I know you're coming home to me every night," she said, placing her free hand on Jessie's cheek.

The bell over the door jingled just as Jessie was about to press her lips to Ellie's. "And thus starts the day," she said with a smile as she backed away and slipped her hat on. She grabbed her mug and a copy of the newspaper sitting nearby. Then, she placed a coin on the counter to cover her purchase.

"Be careful out there," Ellie said, watching her leave as she headed over to greet her customer.

"Always," she replied, nodding to the rancher who'd come into the store, on her way out.

***

Bert was leaning against the doorway of the Marshal's Office, chewing on a licorice stick, when Jessie walked over from the General Trade. She went inside and sat down at her desk with the paper.

"Molly keeps talking about your ceremony, and how lovely it was. I think she's become a fan of outdoor weddings," he said. "It was nice though, I have to agree. We were married in the church back home. Nothing fancy, I suppose, but it was full of family and friends."

"I've been married five times now, and they're all the same to me, but I think this one turned out all right," Jessie replied, sipping her coffee without looking up from the newspaper she was reading. Boone Creek didn't have a local paper, although the mayor had been talking about adding one into the budget, which was obviously a higher priority than adding another deputy or two. Since settling in the town, Jessie had taken to reading the Frontier Ledger, a weekly newspaper out of Red Rock that covered local news, but also reported on major national news when they heard about it.

"What? No—" Bert stammered.

Jessie winked at him and turned the next page. "It can't be," she mumbled, setting the paper down and pulling open her rickety desk drawer. She flipped through a file containing old newspapers and pulled one out. "Son of a bitch!" she growled, wadding up the paper. "I'll be back in a bit," she said to him as she rushed out of the building.

A few town folk greeted her, giving a wave or polite nod as Jessie walked briskly down Main Street Curve, to the large building at the end of the corner. She stepped inside and hurried up the stairs.

"Good afternoon, Jessie," Mayor Montgomery said when she appeared at his office door. "How's married life?"

"It's been less than a week. Ask me in a month," she mumbled. "Do you read the newspaper?" she asked seriously, moving into the room and closing the door.

"We don't currently have one," he replied, puffing on a cigar.

Graysen Morgen

"The Frontier Ledger," she corrected, setting the carelessly folded paper on his desk, before walking over to the window to look down at the street below.

"Of course. Why? What's got you all excited?" He picked it up, glancing at the front cover. "This is two weeks old."

"Page two," she uttered.

He flipped the paper over and glanced at the entries. One entire column was nothing but a listing of trial dates for territory lawbreakers, along with the location of the trial and the charges against them. Shamus Maguire's name was in the very middle.

"Well, son of a bitch," he spat.

"Shamus knew all along that the paper would give his gang exactly what they needed to attack us," she uttered, shaking her head.

"How the hell did we miss this?"

"I knew they listed all of the territory trial information, but I never thought much about it."

"So did I," he stated, blowing out a frustrated breath.

"I never even finished reading this issue because I was dealing with Shamus and his big mouth."

"The front page looks familiar, but I don't get to read them all the way through sometimes. This was probably one of those times, unfortunately."

Jessie sat down in the chair in front of his desk. "I understand the need to inform people, but... something of this nature shouldn't be public knowledge, at least in my opinion. How many other transports have been ambushed because of this, I wonder?"

"I'd like to know the answer to that myself. I'll have a discussion with Justice Samuelson. For now, keep this in a safe place. We'll need it as evidence if this gets messy."

"Do you think it will...get messy?" Jessie asked.

"No," he replied, shaking his head.

***

Later that evening, Jessie sat at her usual table in the back corner of the Rustler's Den. Bert was next to her, tapping his foot to the music of the piano while watching a Faro game.

"Do you think things will be okay with Justice Samuelson?" Bert asked.

"I don't see why not," Jessie said, watching the Dice table. "He's at it again."

"Who? Mr. Munroe?"

"Who else?" she muttered, shaking her head.

"How is he winning so much?"

"He's using weighted dice. When the turn comes to him, he switches the house dice to his own using sleight of hand. It's a fairly simply technique, but the problem is, he does it too often. You're supposed to do it for a few hands, then switch them back so that you lose. Then, switch them and win a few more."

"It sounds like you know a lot about it."

"I've gambled a time or two. I never said I was perfect." She glanced at him. "I had another life before I came here."

"Me too. I worked with Grim and our dad, driving street cars in St. Louis. What about you? What did you do down south?"

"Ran cattle across the Texas/Mexico border."

Bert nodded. "Have you really been married five times?"

"Hell no," she laughed. "This is my first and last."

Bert smiled and shook his head.

"Look, Mr. Munroe is leaving."

"We missed our opportunity."

"We'll get another one," she said.

He watched the saloon girls go around the room, working each table. "I guess Miss Lita isn't hanging all over our table anymore, now that you're married."

"No, it's not that...I'm pretty sure she hates me," she replied, laughing lightly. "Mr. Munroe is gone and it's starting to quiet down. I'm going to call it a night," she added, standing up.

"Me too. I'll see you tomorrow."

Jessie patted his shoulder and walked up to the bar.

"That damn Nicolas Munroe has been in here all day, challenging anyone who will play, and taking their money of course," Elmer spat. "What are you going to do about it?"

"I'll bust him soon enough," she said.

"The town folk are going to catch on, then they'll fill him full of holes."

"I know. At least we are doing well with the no carry law. I'll stop him before it gets to that point."

"Yeah, like you stopped 'High Card' Jack or the Dirty Boys?" Otis mumbled. "Lady Law," he laughed.

"Otis, you're lucky I'm in a good mood and ready to go home to my wife. Otherwise, I'd toss your scrawny ass outside," she said.

"A woman isn't allowed to marry no woman. That pastor's done lost his mind." He shook his head, nearly falling off the stool as he reached for his drink.

"Elmer, he's done for the night. Cut him off," she said.

"Oh, come on! Now, you're going to tell us how much we can drink? What's next? Are you going to measure it while I take a piss?" he growled.

"Otis! Now, that's enough!" Elmer yelled. "She's still a lady and you don't talk like that to a lady."

"It's okay," Jessie said, holding her hand up to Elmer. "I'm about as far from a proper lady as you can get, but he's right," she said, looking at Otis. "Your mouth is going to dig you a hole that you can't climb out of."

"What are you going to do? Arrest me? I haven't broken any rules. Leave me the hell alone," he growled.

Jessie shook her head. "Keep an eye on him. I mean it, no more drinks tonight," she said to Elmer. "I'm heading home."

He watched her leave before walking back over to Otis, taking his glass away. "That woman doesn't play around. I suggest you stop harassing her," he said.

"She doesn't scare me," he sneered.

"She ought to," Elmer sighed and continued in a serious tone, "She's done a lot of good around here, and all you do is poke her with a sharp stick every time she comes near. I personally don't want to see what happens when you finally do piss her off, and I'm pretty sure you don't want to either."

Otis huffed angrily as he stumbled off the stool and stormed out.

***

It was dark in the General Store when Jessie walked inside. She struck a match and lit a walking candle so she could find her way up the stairs. Ellie was asleep in the bed when she stepped into the room. After splashing some water on her face at the washing bowl, she removed her clothes, relieved herself in the chamber pot, and climbed into the bed.

Ellie slept with her hair in a long braid so that she could easily move, leaving the soft skin of her neck exposed. Jessie cuddled close, pressing her lips to the delicate area. Ellie stirred, then rolled in her direction.

"How was your night?" she whispered.

"Quiet." Jessie wrapped her arms around Ellie. "Lying here with you feels like a dream," she said, pulling her close.

"Then I don't ever want to wake up," Ellie murmured, kissing her softly.

"Me either," Jessie replied, rolling her to her back and deepening the kiss.

TWENTY-ONE

Justice Walker T. Samuelson arrived in town a few days later on a stage out of Red Rock. He was taller than Jessie expected, and slightly round in the midsection. His gray hair was oiled and perfectly combed, and his matching mustache was twisted into two long, straight lines over his upper lip. He wore a dark suit with a light gray vest, a black puff-tie, and a bowler hat.

"You must be the Town Marshal, Jessie Henry," he said, holding out his hand.

"Yes, Sir," she replied. "This is my deputy, Bert."

"Nice to meet you both." He looked around, pursing his lips. "Where's Mayor Montgomery?"

"In his office. He sent us to escort you over."

"Well, now...I've been here before. I'm sure I can find my way. That is...unless, it's dangerous on the street in the middle of the day?"

"Oh, no Sir. Boone Creek is a safe place. If you'd like to go on your own, simply take Main Street here, all the way to the end where it turns into Main Street Curve. Follow that around and you'll see his office on the left hand side," she stated.

"I'll do that," he said. "How about you two meet me at the mayor's office in a couple of hours, say four o'clock?"

"Sure thing. Enjoy your stay here in Boone Creek," Jessie replied with a smile as she tipped her hat to him.

Bert stood next to her as they watched the man walk away. "I have a feeling I'm not going to like him," he whispered.

Jessie laughed. "Bert, you like everyone."

"That's not true."

"Name me one person you don't like." She crossed her arms and waited.

He thought for a minute, switching his weight from one foot to the other.

"See, I told you. Come on, it's hot as hell out here," she said, wiping the sweat from her brow. They'd started leaving their coats behind in the middle of the day, due to the summer heat, but with the justice in town, they'd kept them on.

As they passed by the theatre, Jessie looked over at the Closed sign and sighed.

"I wonder if it will ever reopen," Bert muttered.

"Not as long as that clown, Nicolas Munroe, is pretending to buy it." She shook her head. "It could be a great establishment for this town."

"It used to be, before the thugs took over the town. Molly and I went there a time or two to see the shows."

"I was hoping I'd see you," Ellie called from the sidewalk of the General Trade, where she was cleaning the outside of the store windows. "I made fresh biscuits with honey jam." She smiled.

"Perfect timing, I'm starved," Jessie said, kissing her cheek as she passed by and stepped inside the store.

"Bert, you're welcome to have some, but you better hurry. She'll eat them all before you get a bite."

"Molly sent me with small cakes this morning," he replied.

"I'll have to trade recipes with her."

"She'd love that, Mrs. Henry."

Jessie walked back outside a minute later with her mouth full of biscuit and another one in her hand. "Here," she said, handing one to Bert. "Try this."

"I'm fine. I ate all of those small cakes this morning."

"Oh, eat the damn biscuit, Bert," Jessie retorted.

Ellie covered her mouth with her hand as she bit back a laugh.

"This is delicious," he mumbled between bites. "You simply must trade recipes. I'll let her know this evening."

"Sure thing, but only if you stop calling me Mrs. Henry," she chided. "You were in my wedding for crying out loud. I consider you and Molly my friends."

Bert smiled and nodded politely.

"I saw the justice arrived a bit ago. He stopped in for a tin of tea leaves on his way to see the mayor."

"Did you give him the mint ones?"

"No. I ran out a few days ago. He was looking specifically for peach leaves, said his wife loves peach tea, but I've never had any in here. Apparently, they've been out of them for a while in Red Rock. He was trying to surprise her, I suppose." She finished the window and carried her washing stuff inside.

"Speaking of Justice Samuelson, we're meeting with him and the mayor in a little bit. I'm not sure how long we'll be, but I'll come for supper afterwards."

"That's fine." She smiled, dabbing the sweat from her forehead onto a towel.

"Let's have another walk around town before we have to head over there," Jessie said to Bert.

***

Some of the town folk waved, others stopped to say hi as Bert and Jessie made their rounds. Otis stood outside of the saloon, mumbling something as they passed.

"Why does that old drunk hate you so much?" Bert questioned. "I don't remember him giving Marshal Milford a hard time, then again, everyone pretty much walked all over him."

"Maybe that's what it is. I uphold the law and bring order to the town. Or, he could just hate women. I couldn't care less," she replied, pulling a cigar from her pocket. She struck the match on the bottom of her boot and lit it with ease.

"Marshal Henry," Pastor Noah said, nodding in her direction as they passed by the church. "How's married life treating you?"

"Pretty good so far," she called.

"That's grand," he replied. "I'm looking forward to seeing you on Sunday. I hope you have your spot all picked out."

"Sure do," she answered as they kept walking.

"What was that all about? You don't go to church."

"Oh, just a little deal I struck with the pastor, and no...I do not go to church."

As they went further around the corner, Bert could see his house, which sat closer to where Center Street cut through town. He waved to Molly, who was sitting out on the small front porch.

"Do you want to walk down and say hi before we go in?" Jessie asked.

"No. Let's get this over with," he said, looking in that direction one more time. "She's been talking about having kids."

"Oh..." Jessie nodded.

"What about you and Ellie? Do you want kids?"

"Well..." Jessie cleared her throat and snubbed out the remainder of her cigar. "That would be something of a miracle, I believe."

"I know that, I mean is it something you want?"

"We've been married all of a week. Kids haven't exactly been part of our conversations." She looked up at the sky. "I never really knew my father and my mother was harlot, so I'm not sure how I'd be any different in the long run."

Bert raised his brows in surprise.

"What about you?" Jessie asked.

"I don't know. I suppose I'd be a pretty good father. I know Molly would be a wonderful mother."

"Marshal, Deputy, glad you could join us," Mayor Montgomery said, opening the door to his office after seeing them milling about out front.

"We're a tad bit early," Jessie replied, removing her hat and walking up the stairs.

"It's fine. We were just waiting for you two to arrive," the mayor said, walking alongside her.

"Good to see you again, Marshal Henry, Deputy Bert." Justice Samuelson shook their hands when they entered the mayor's office. "Please, have a seat," he added, waving to the extra chairs in front of the mayor's desk.

Bert sat next to Jessie, who was next to the justice. The mayor sat in his chair on the opposite side.

Graysen Morgen

"I'm going to get right to the point. There's no sense in wasting either of your time. When a felon, that's what we call them in the justice system, dies in the jail while awaiting trial, or during transport to his trial, the court system must complete a thorough review of those events, which is why I am here. Now, Shamus Maguire was in your care from May 14th until June 3rd, is that correct?"

"Yes," Jessie answered. "We left for Red Rock the morning of June third."

"Did he have any visitors during this time?"

"No. We don't allow jailers to be visited."

"Okay. That sounds a bit harsh, but nonetheless, did you see or overhear anyone talking about Mr. Maguire? Perhaps in the saloon or on the streets?"

"There was some talk, but I wasn't involved with any of it."

"All right. Take me through June third."

Together, Bert and Jessie gave a recount of the ambush, the roundup of the bodies, and their return to Boone Creek.

"Do you have any idea where the other four men came from? Or how they knew where to find you?" he asked.

"They came up on us from behind, but they could've come from anywhere," Bert said.

"They knew where we'd be and when we'd be there because of this," Jessie stated, handing him the Frontier Ledger. "Turn to page two."

Justice Samuelson glanced at the mayor, then flipped the paper over.

"That list right there on the left is all of your felons and their trial dates. Shamus's gang could've read that and lied in wait, knowing how long it would take to get to

163

Red Rock from Boone Creek, as well as the path we'd take. We pretty much handed ourselves to them."

"Justice, I'd like to know how many transports have been ambushed in the past six months," Mayor Montgomery chimed in. "I believe this list is putting sheriffs and marshals in jeopardy out in the open terrain, and thus should be stopped at once."

"Well, now, Mayor, we can't just shut down the newspaper."

"I'm not saying the paper, but this column should cease. Aren't our law officer's lives more important than the criminals?"

"Part of a law officer's job is to protect the criminals while they're in custody."

"I agree, but who is going to protect our law officers?" the mayor asked.

"This information is printed in the newspaper because the public has a right to know about these upcoming trials. It's the only way to inform everyone at the same time. We simply can't wire everyone who may wish to witness one of these trials. Therefore, we put it the newspaper."

Mayor Montgomery shook his head. "Bert and Jessie, will you step out in the hall for a minute?"

Jessie nodded and stood up. Bert followed her out of the room.

"You want to shoot that ridiculous mustache off his face, don't you?" he said.

"What gives you that idea?" She grinned.

"He can't honestly think we planned this whole thing."

"Of course he doesn't. He knows the truth. Since they advertise all of the trial information in the paper like it's news, I'm sure this isn't the first time a transport has been attacked. He just won't admit it. He's here using his authority to stroke his own ego at our expense," she spat.

Bert shook his head in disgust. "I would like to see what happens when he's the one out there dodging bullets, and getting dragged by buggy, while a bunch of madmen are trying to kill him!"

"He'd piss all over himself," she laughed.

***

The mayor waited for Jessie and Bert to leave his office, then he continued. "Walt, no disrespect. You're an old friend. I've known you since before you became a judge. You and I both know my marshal and deputy had nothing to do with Shamus Maguire's death, or the deaths of his gang members. They were attacked and fought back to save their own lives."

"I'm not disagreeing with you, Horace. I'm sure they read about the trial and planned the ambush all along, but there are laws in place, which I must follow, and one of them is conducting a full review on a situation such as this one. You know we've had sheriffs and marshals taking the law into their own hands for far too long. This new law is to hold them accountable for their behavior, and help prevent it from happening."

"I understand. Where do we go from here? You have their statements."

"I need to see the wagon, and we'll have to exhume the bodies."

"What on earth for?" Mayor Montgomery barked.

"I need to see how they died."

"For crying out loud, they were shot. What more do you need to see? Our town doctor looked over them before they were buried. Maybe he can give you his statement, instead of digging them up. I'm all for justice, but this is taking things a little too far, in my opinion."

"I know you well, and I know you won't purposely steer me wrong. Let's look at the wagon and talk with the doctor. If everything checks out, I won't have the bodies exhumed. Deal?"

"Fine." Mayor Montgomery stood up. "The wagon is in the stable," he said, before pulling his office door open. "Come on. We're going to see the wagon," he stated to Jessie and Bert as he put his hat on.

They both nodded, following behind the men as they made their way out of the building and down the street. No words were exchanged as they walked along.

***

"Mayor," the stable-hand said cheerfully. "What can I do for you?"

"We need to see the wagon from the ambush."

"It's in the back here. We have it on the repair schedule, but were told to hold off until you gave the go ahead."

"That's correct," Mayor Montgomery replied. "We were waiting for this man, Justice Walter T. Samuelson. He's here to have a look at it."

"Well, right here it is." He pulled the cloth covering back, revealing the bullet riddled and bloodied wagon.

"My word," Justice Samuelson gasped. He walked around, taking in the array of holes, and noticed the blood stains in the back. "This will do for now. I'll speak with the doctor in the morning, and let you know of my decision," he said, looking at the mayor.

"All right. Do you know your way to the hotel?"

"We can escort you, if you'd like," Jessie said.

"I'll be fine," he replied. "Have a good evening."

Jessie watched him walk away. "I thought this wasn't supposed to get messy?"

"It's not. He's just doing his job. The justice department is trying to put a stop to Frontier Law."

"Why is he meeting with Doc Vernon?" Bert asked.

"He wants to dig up the Dirty Boys' bodies."

"What the hell for?"

"To see their bullet holes, I guess," he sighed. "After seeing his reaction to the wagon, I doubt he'll go any further. But, it's best that you both be available in the morning anyhow."

"We'll call it an early night, tonight," Jessie said.

***

Jessie was sitting at the dining table in the room above the General Trade, which they called home, eating eggs and biscuits with honey jam. She smiled at Ellie when she handed her a cup of coffee and sat down.

"I don't see how digging up those men has any merit. They tried to kill you and Bert. The holes in the wagon are proof of that," she said. "He might as well let them rest in hell where they belong."

Jessie raised a brow, but didn't say anything.

The bell above the door down below, rang loudly, indicating someone had walked into the store.

"Marshal!" Bert called.

"He must have news," Jessie said. "Be down in a minute!" she yelled, grabbing a biscuit to go. "I love you. I'll let know what's going on as soon as I can." She softly kissed Ellie's lips and grabbed her hat before rushing down the stairs.

"Justice Samuelson left on a stage ten minutes ago," Bert exclaimed.

"What?"

"I saw it with my own eyes."

"All right," she said between bites of biscuit. "Let's go find the mayor and see what the hell is going on."

* * *

"I was just coming to see you," Mayor Montgomery said, meeting them in the street outside of the Marshal's Office, across from the General Trade. "Justice Samuelson left a little bit ago after finishing his inquiry."

"That's it? I thought he was meeting with Doc Vernon?" Jessie asked.

"He decided he didn't need to."

"I'm glad he's out of the picture...what about the newspaper column?"

"It's a public service announcement. He won't budge on changing it, and he won't give me the details on the number of transports that have been attacked."

"I thought you two were friends?" she questioned.

"We go way back, but he's a territory justice, and with that comes a little arrogance and a lot of power. They walk a fine line, just like any politician."

"Remind me never to get into politics," Jessie mumbled. The mayor laughed. "You'd never be able to walk that fine of a line."

"You've got that right," she said.

TWENTY-TWO

Jessie held Ellie's hand as she walked next to her. "Keep your eyes closed," she said, watching the ground to make sure she didn't trip.

"I am," Ellie replied excitedly.

The large tree they were married under came into view as they crossed over the streaming creek. A blanket was spread out on the ground in the spot where they'd had the ceremony, with a picnic basket sitting on the corner.

"Okay," Jessie blurted when they were only a few feet away.

"Oh, my!" Ellie beamed. "What is all of this for?"

"It's been three weeks since we stood here and committed our lives to each other. I know things have been a bit crazy, with the justice in town last week, and all of that, but I wanted you to know how much you mean to me."

"This is so sweet of you." Ellie kissed her cheek before sitting on the blanket and tucking her legs under her.

Jessie sat down next to her and opened the basket, pulling out a large slice of brandied peach pie and two forks.

Ellie laughed. "I remember you bringing this to me in the store."

"I also have this," Jessie said, removing a flask and pouring the liquid into two mugs.

"Is that mint tea?"

"Sure is."

"Where did you get that? I ran out of those leaves a while ago."

"It just so happens Miss Mable didn't use all of her leaves. She made tea for the girls, then hid the rest for herself."

"How did you know this? Have you been hanging around that place?"

"Of course not. She is my friend, Ellie. That's not going to change. However, the mayor told me. I happened to ask him if he'd bought any tea leaves recently, and he told me about this wonderful tea that she'd made for him when he visited last. So, I went to see if she had anymore, and she did."

Ellie nodded.

"I'd never step out on you, Ellie. That I promise."

"I believe you, and I know you'd never lie to me."

Jessie picked up a cup of tea, handing it to her, before grabbing the other one for herself. "You know, I fell in love with you the day you made this for me...even if it wasn't for me."

Ellie smiled. "Can I tell you a secret? It really was for you. I got nervous and said it wasn't."

"I knew it!" Jessie exclaimed, shaking her head.

"I fell for you over this pie though," Ellie said, taking a bite. "I couldn't believe you'd brought it to share with me. No one has ever done that before. I knew then that I couldn't say no if you ever asked for my hand."

Jessie wrapped her arm around her and leaned closer, kissing her softly as the sun began to set over the mountain in the distance.

"If I'd known it was this beautiful out here, I would've picked sunset for our ceremony, instead of noon. It looks like someone reached up and painted the sky," Ellie whispered.

"I've seen some of the most stunning sunsets over the years, but nothing compares to this one, right now," Jessie said, holding her close. "Can I ask you something?" she murmured.

"Sure." Ellie smiled.

"Why didn't you and your husband have any kids?"

Ellie stiffened in her arms. "I...uh...we wanted them," she muttered, "we tried, but it didn't happen," she sighed. "Why? Do you want kids?"

"It's just something Bert was going on about." Jessie kissed the side of her cheek. "Besides, us having a kid together is impossible."

"I accepted that I couldn't have kids back when it didn't happen for Corny and I. So, when I agreed to marry you, the idea of having them, never crossed my mind."

Jessie felt Ellie relax once more as they watched the sun's rays, disappear into the mountain.

***

As soon as the sun was completely gone, they packed up and headed home. "There's something else I want to show you," Jessie said, helping Ellie out of her clothes.

Graysen Morgen

"Oh, really? And what might that be?" Ellie asked playfully as she began unbuttoning Jessie's vest.

"You'll have to wait and find out," Jessie teased.

With their clothing removed, the two women stepped over to the bed, trading kisses along the way. Ellie lie down on her side, and Jessie mimicked her position. Gentle kisses turned into passionate lip locks with wandering hands and tender touches.

"Are you ready for me to show you?" Jessie whispered, nibbling her ear.

"Yes," she exhaled.

Jessie rolled Ellie to her back and got on top of her. They shared another heated kiss before Jessie moved down, tracing a path across Ellie's chest with her tongue, circling her nipples before sucking them between her lips.

Ellie tried to control her labored breathing as she watched her work lower, gliding her tongue over her stomach, then down to her hips, before pushing her legs further apart.

Jessie looked up at Ellie, meeting her eyes as she softly ran her tongue over the glistening folds.

"My God!" Ellie cried out.

Jessie kept going, adding a little more pressure with each passing stroke, back and forth. Ellie writhed under her with her body out of control. Her head was spinning, her spine trembling, and her heart thumping like it was about to jump right out of her chest. She feared she wouldn't get enough air, she was breathing so fast, as she put her hand over her mouth, trying to quell her moaning, but in the end, she just didn't care. Her body had never felt anything like what it was going through at that moment.

173

Jessie held her thighs apart and slipped her tongue inside of Ellie, thrusting in and out, before going back to her center, licking in lazy circles. She continued the same pattern of circles and thrusts until Ellie tightened like an extended rubber band. Pulling away, she kissed the same pattern back up her body, stopping at Ellie's lips, where they shared a sultry kiss.

Ellie leaned back slightly, still breathless. "I've never...no one's ever..." she tried to speak. "What was that?"

"Another part of making love," Jessie whispered, kissing her again.

"I have no idea what you even did."

Jessie smiled. "I can do it again, if you want."

"Please do," Ellie murmured.

***

A summer rainstorm passed over the next couple of days, dropping a lot of rain and bringing heavy winds that caused some damage on a few buildings, and large pot holes to form in the street. Mayor Montgomery worked a deal with the miners to make the repairs to the street, while business owners had to fend for themselves, making their own building repairs. Luckily, Jessie and Ellie had gotten away unscathed, as the General Trade was well built. The Marshal's Office, however, wasn't so lucky. They'd gotten a roof leak at some point, causing some flooding in the jail cells. The mayor also had the miners make those repairs.

By the time things settled back down again, it was the fourth of July and everyone was having a good time, which meant Bert and Jessie were on high alert.

"There's no telling who snuck in a gun to shoot it off," she said as they entered the Rustler's Den, which was crowded with people. Couples danced to the piano tune, and gamblers crammed around the Faro game and Dice table. The rest of the patrons were either lining the bar or gathered around the sitting tables. Jessie's usual table was occupied, so she and Bert stood with their backs to the wall, near the bar.

"Coffee?" Elmer asked loudly.

"Not yet," she answered, scanning the large room.

Lita was on the dance floor with a rancher, spinning around and twirling her cinched skirt. Seeing Jessie looking her way, she began moving provocatively against the man, who seemed to be enjoying every minute of their dance.

Jessie continued observing the room, barely noticing the harlot who was trying to get her attention. She motioned for Bert to check the Faro game, while she moved closer to the Dice table, both searching for hidden guns.

"Come on lucky eight! Who's with me?" Nicolas Munroe cheered. He was leading the charge as the castor at the Dice table, rolling winner after winner, around a pile of silver trade dollars. After another winning roll, which gave him the pile of coins, a few players started making comments.

Jessie moved in closer, as if she were about to set down money to play, but she snatched the dice up instead, just before Nicolas could retrieve them with the dice stick.

"Hey!" he protested. "Wait your turn, Marshal!"

"Your turn is over, Mr. Munroe," she said, examining the dice. Sure enough, they were not the house dice with the letters RD etched on the side with one dot.

"Excuse me? You can't come into a middle of a game and decide when someone's turn is over. Don't you know the rules, or do you just do whatever you want and take what isn't yours?" he spat.

"I suggest you leave for the night and cool off. We don't need any trouble in here," she replied.

Bert stepped up beside her as backup.

"You're the one causing trouble. We're playing a game here, Marshal!" one of the men yelled.

"The only person playing a game here is Mr. Munroe. He's been running a scam on you all evening." She held up the dice. "These are not house dice. In fact, they're weighted to specifically land on the numbers he chooses."

"You hustling piece of shit!" one man yelled, lurching at Nicolas.

"She's lying!" Nicolas spat. "You're going to believe this good-for-nothing, with no morals, over me? I've been playing this game with you boys for weeks. We're all friends here. You know me. What do you know about her? Other than she steps in where she doesn't belong and isn't wanted."

"I've had about enough of your mouth," she yelled yanking him out of his seat, shaking his arm sleeves in the process. two white dice flopped out of his left sleeve, rolling to a stop in the middle of the table. Jessie grabbed them, noticing the etching marks when she turned them over in her hand. "Gentlemen, these are the house dice."

"You son of a bitch!" one of the guys shouted, lurching for Nicolas.

Bert held him back.

Jessie stuffed the cheating dice in her vest pocket. "Mr. Munroe, it's best that you leave this town, preferably tonight. Otherwise, I'm going to lock your ass in the jail until you shrivel up into nothing, you spineless weasel!" she growled, shoving him through the crowd. "Get your ass out of my sight!"

Players of the game cheered while other saloon patrons questioned what was happening.

"Bert, split this pot between all of those men who were sitting here playing with him," she said.

He nodded and began counting as she walked over to the bar.

"It's about time you threw him out of here. I was afraid one of those miner boys would kill him if he won anymore rounds," Elmer said, shaking his head. "I figured you were about ready for this," he added, sliding a cup of coffee to her.

"They probably will anyway, if he doesn't leave town," she replied, reaching for the mug.

Bert finished divvying up the coins and left the table with the house dice so they could restart their game.

"What a mess," he said, walking up next to her at the bar. "Do you think he will leave?"

"If he knows what's good for him, he will."

"Jessie Henry, I'm calling you out!" Nicolas Munroe shouted from outside the saloon, shooting his pistol once in the air. The sound of the gunshot grabbed everyone's attention.

"He's lost his mind," Elmer muttered.

"You took her from me and you know it!" he continued yelling from the street. "She was going to marry me!" He shot again.

"You think you're a man, come on out here and stand up to me like a man!" He holstered his pistol, walking closer to the saloon doors. "I'm calling you out, you coward!"

"What are you going to do?" Bert asked.

"I've enough of this shit for one night," Jessie growled.

Everyone watched as she turned and walked out the door. Bert rushed after her for backup, but it was too late. Jessie drew her gun, firing in Nicolas' direction before she was even off the sidewalk. The bullet blew through the center of his top hat, knocking it off his head. Nicolas dove to the ground, wide-eyed with fear.

"You just tried to kill me!"

"If I'd wanted you dead, you'd be dead," she said in a low, menacing tone. "Give me that gun before I shoot it off you!"

With shaking hands, he pulled his pistol, handing her the butt of it.

"I ought to pistol whip you with your own gun!" She shook her head. "Get on a horse."

"What horse?"

"Any God damn horse!" She spread her hands around to the array of horses tied to hitching posts. "Pick one and ride off, right now before I change my mind. If I ever see your sorry ass again, or I hear of you uttering a word about my wife or my marriage, I *will* shoot you dead. Do you hear me?"

Nicolas nodded.

"Now!" she shouted.

He jumped up off the ground, running to the nearest horse.

"What you just did is illegal. You can't threaten a man's life because he said something that hurt your feelings," Otis muttered from a few feet away.

Jessie drew her gun, aiming it straight at his head.

"Whoa!" he gasped, throwing his hands up. 'I'm unarmed! You all see this, she's trying to shoot an unarmed man!"

"Oh, for God's sake, Otis!" she spat. "Put your damn hands down." She flipped her gun around so that she was holding the barrel as she stepped close to him. "If you don't stop with your insults, I'm going to pistol whip you," she said low enough for only him to hear. "When I'm finished, you're going to wish I *had* shot you instead." She holstered her gun, then pretended to draw it quickly, but only used her hand as a gun when she pointed it at him.

Otis jumped back, thinking she was going to shoot him, and landed on his butt in the horse trough. Everyone laughed.

"Serves you right, you old drunken bag of bones!" she chuckled as she went back inside the saloon. "Come on, folks. Show's over."

"You scare me sometimes," Bert said, shaking his head.

"Why? Did you really think I was going to kill Mr. Munroe or actually shoot Otis?"

"I knew you wouldn't, but I felt like you might."

She shrugged. "You're right, a person can only take so much. If you don't show authority, you will get run over time and time again." She grabbed her coffee mug, taking a sip. "Besides, I've told you before, I take personal threats on my life seriously. Now, him running off at the mouth about Ellie, that's just something you

179

don't do. When you speak ill of someone's wife, that's as good as calling them out."

"I agree. If someone ever spoke ill of Molly, I...I'm not sure what I'd do," Bert replied.

***

Jessie spent the next morning explaining her actions to the mayor. He agreed that tossing Mr. Munroe out of town was a wise decision, albeit he wasn't too happy about her way of going about it.

On her way back to the Marshal's Office, she noticed Ellie standing outside, peering down the street in the opposite direction.

"Looking for someone?" Jessie called.

Ellie spun around, holding her hand up to mask the sun shining in her eyes. 'There you are!" she exclaimed, holding her skirt up as she rushed over to her. "What's this I hear about you shooting Mr. Munroe last night? You only said things got out of hand at the saloon."

"They did...or rather he did."

"So, you shot him?"

"I didn't shoot him...I scared him. He deserved to be shot, though."

"What's that supposed to mean?" Ellie questioned.

"He's a no-good scoundrel, and we didn't need him in this town."

"There goes the only buyer for the theatre," she muttered, shaking her head.

"You don't believe me?"

"I don't know what to believe. Since when do you go around shooting at people? I heard you shot at Otis, too!"

"I did no such thing. I drew my hand like a gun and he was so drunk and paranoid, he fell in the horse trough."

Ellie tried not to laugh. "Well, you still shot at Mr. Munroe."

"He called me outside, planning to shoot me first! Or did whoever gossiped to you forget that part?"

"I didn't hear that."

"I'm sure you didn't. He was out in the street, shooting his pistol like a buffoon, yelling for me to come outside and face him. He said you wanted to marry him, but I asked first, stealing you away. Is that true?"

Ellie furrowed her brow.

"It is, isn't it? That's why you're mad that I shot at him and ran him out of town.

"No. Of course not. He was nice and had a lot of great ideas for the theatre and this town."

"He was a hustler who had been swindling people's money for weeks by cheating them at dice!" Jessie shook her head. "Were you sweet on him, Ellie?"

"I'm appalled that you would even ask me that. I'm your wife!" she huffed, crossing her arms.

"Well, why are you so mad at me for doing my job?"

"Because I don't want you to get killed," Ellie yelled. "You always seem to be right in the middle of danger…with the outlaws, and now with Mr. Munroe."

"I'm fine. I can handle the outlaws and whatever else comes my way. That's why I'm the marshal."

"Well…I'm not sure I can handle it," Ellie stated.

Jessie clenched her jaw. She had no idea where the conversation was headed, but the last thing she wanted to hear was regret in Ellie's voice. "I have work to do," she said, walking away before anymore words were spoken.

Leaving the Marshal's Office behind her, she headed down the street towards the Rustler's Den.

Elmer was behind the bar, drying freshly washed glasses with a hand towel, when she walked in.

"Afternoon, Marshal."

"Pour me a whiskey," she said, sitting on a stool.

"In the middle of the day?"

"Pour it, Elmer."

He obliged, turning over one of the fresh glasses and filling it halfway with rusty-looking, brown liquid. "Anything you want to talk about?" he asked, sliding it over to her.

She knocked the double shot back and set the glass down.

"Does this have anything to do with last night?"

Jessie nodded.

"The mayor can be a real stick in the mud sometimes. You might have gone a little over the top, but you got your point across. If he wants law and order in this town, he needs to let you do your job."

"It's not him, although we hashed things out this morning," she said.

"Then, who is it?"

"Ellie."

Elmer pursed his lips and nodded.

"She's upset with me for the way I handled things with Nicolas Munroe. I was only doing my job. I'm beginning to wonder if he was right."

"I first met that young woman when she came to town on the arm of her new husband, Cornelius Fray. Now, don't get me wrong, she was happy, but there was no light in her eyes like I saw the day she married you, Marshal. She loves you, there's no denying that. I also

Graysen Morgen

saw her bury her husband, which certainly wasn't easy. She worries about you and is concerned for your safety. Can you blame her, after what she's been through? It doesn't mean she fancies someone else," he said. "Go to your wife and talk this out with her. Sitting here drinking in the middle of the day isn't going to fix it."

Jessie knew he was right. She placed a coin on the bar to cover her drink, and left.

***

Ellie was standing in the store when Jessie walked in, removing her hat.

"Can we talk?" she said.

"I don't like that you walked away."

"I know."

Ellie moved closer. "I'm happy that you're cleaning up the town, Jessie. No one here hates the outlaws more than me, but I don't want you to lose your life in the process," she said. "The outlaws have taken everything from me. I couldn't bear them taking you, too," she sobbed.

Jessie pulled Ellie into her arms. "Hey…it's okay. I'm right here. No one is taking me away from you, not now, not ever."

"There's so much you don't know."

"So, tell me," Jessie said.

"My husband, Corny, was shot and killed right here on this very street. In front of the theatre, to be exact," she mumbled against Jessie's neck. "A couple of outlaws were fighting with a local rancher. Being the nice guy that he was, Corny went outside to see what was going on and help break it up. The outlaw shot him square in the chest," she sniffed as a few more tears fell. "I hate them," she bawled, pounding on Ellie's chest as all of the resentment she'd buried, rose to the surface. "As far as I'm concerned, they should all be dead. Every last person who calls them self an outlaw should be shot or hung, or both. They're ruthless, vicious, people who will take anything and everything from you," she continued, letting it all out.

Jessie held her as she cried, wondering if marrying Ellie was the right thing to do. The last thing she'd ever want to do was break her heart.

"I'm sorry," Ellie said, pulling herself somewhat together.

"It's okay."

"I didn't mean to put all of that on you. I know you have a job to do...I just...hearing about the shooting brought it all back to the surface. I hadn't thought about Corny or that day in a long time. I guess it's because I'm married to you now, and you deal with that dangerous nonsense almost daily," she said, drying her face.

"I do. You're right, but you have to trust that I know what I'm doing, especially when it comes to lawbreakers."

"You're the best marshal this town has ever had," Ellie said with a smile. "I can't fault you for that."

"No, you can't." Jessie grinned.

"You smell like whiskey. Let me guess, you went to talk to Elmer."

"I did. Why? Where would you go if you needed to talk something out?"

"To Pastor Noah, of course."

Jessie smiled and shook her head.

"You should come inside with me one day. I think you'd like his sermons better if you could hear them."

"I heard the one this past week just fine from outside."

Ellie laughed and kissed her cheek. "I should get supper started."

"Let's go to the Kettle Kitchen tonight."

"Are you sure?"

"Absolutely."

"Only if we can share a piece of pie."

"Deal," Jessie said, kissing her lips.

TWENTY-THREE

The sweltering summer sun beat down on her back as Jessie walked around the prairie, picking wild flowers. It was barely ten a.m. and sweat was already beading on her forehead and neck. She looked down at the western wallflowers, blue flax flowers, and yellow dandelion flowers, creating a colorful bouquet as she pulled the stems together, tying a ribbon tightly around the cluster.

She made a clicking noise with her mouth and waited a couple of seconds for her brown mare to come over from the nearby grass it had been grazing on. Stowing the flowers in the satchel on the saddle, she climbed up and trotted off, guiding the large animal back to town.

Ellie was standing in the doorway of her store, fanning herself, when Jessie rode up.

"What are you up to?" she asked, raising a brow.

"I was out riding around the outskirts of town," Jessie replied getting down. "I thought I'd bring you something."

"Oh, really?" Ellie closed the fan and stepped closer, trying to peer into the saddle bag as Jessie opened it.

"Hey! No peeking!" Jessie blurted, shooing her away. "Close your eyes."

"What for?"

"Just do it."

"Fine. It better not be a dead animal for me to cook," she huffed with her hands on her hips.

Jessie pulled the flowers out and held them in front of her. "Okay."

Ellie opened her eyes. "Oh, my. These are beautiful." She held them to her nose, inhaling the sweet scent. "And they smell divine." She smiled and leaned in, quickly kissing Jessie's lips, before putting some space between them.

"It's been two months since we were married. I figured flowers as beautiful as you, were as good a gift as anything," Jessie said.

"I'm not sure I deserve you," Ellie sighed. "I was beginning to think being in love wasn't meant for me."

"Why do you say that?"

"I don't know...being a widow puts doubt in your mind, I guess."

"Well, if there's anyone who isn't deserving, it's me. I thought my luck had run out a long time ago, even then...it wasn't really luck," Jessie mumbled. "Anyway, I wanted to give you these and tell you I was thinking about you."

"You made my day a whole lot better." Ellie smiled, smelling the flowers again.

Jessie grinned and mounted the horse. She reached down, petting the mare gently. "I better get her back to the stable. Bert's probably looking for me, anyway. I'll see you later for supper."

"Be safe," Ellie called.

"Always," she replied as she slapped the reins to get the horse moving.

***

Jessie was surprised to see that Bert wasn't at the office when she walked inside. It looked as if he hadn't yet been there, and it was nearly noon. Figuring he may be out looking for her, and there was no sense in both of them wandering around in different directions, she pulled a cigar from her pocket and struck a match along the wall behind her desk. After lighting her smoke, she sat down at her desk with the newspaper.

She'd barely made it through page two when she heard boot steps on the wooden sidewalk. The door was already open, in the hopes that a rare breeze might blow in. Jessie folded the paper to the side when Bert walked in and plopped down in a nearby chair with his shoulders sagging.

"Are you just now coming on duty?" she asked.

"I had a long night," he sighed.

"Everything okay?"

"Yes…no. Hell, I don't know." Bert looked like he was functioning, but his mind was somewhere else.

Jessie raised a brow.

"Molly's been getting sick off and on for a couple of weeks, and it came on pretty strong last night. She's throwing up everything she eats, and running a little fever."

"I'm sorry to hear that. Did Doc Vernon see her?"

"Yeah, he just left the house a bit ago."

"And?" Jessie waited. She was pretty sure she knew the answer. She'd had a feeling for a couple of weeks ever since Bert began querying her about kids, because Molly was questioning him.

Bert opened his mouth and closed it. Then, he looked up at her and said, "She's with child."

"Well, congratulations!" she said with a smile.

He simply nodded.

"You're going to be a father, Bert. Why do you look like your dog died?"

"Back home, Molly had a best friend named Beatrice. She died during child birth. It nearly broke Molly. That's part of the reason we left with my cousin Grim. She was heartbroken and everything reminded her of Bea. She says she'll be fine, and Doc Vernon thinks she's in great health, but I can't help but worry."

Jessie wasn't quite sure what to say to him. She figured Pastor Noah would be a lot better at offering assurance. "If Doc Vernon says she will be okay, then you have to put your trust in him. I know you go to church every week, so you must have faith in God and everything. Now is the time to lean on that, when you need it the most," she finally said.

"Yeah."

"Does Molly know how you feel? Is she worried, too?"

"No. She's over the moon with happiness. If it's a girl, we're going to name her Beatrice," he said as a tear rolled down his cheek. "I can't let her see how scared I am. She needs to be strong and stay healthy." He put his chin to his chest, staring at the floor. "I can't lose her, Marshal. I just can't."

"And you won't. You have to believe that. How far along is she?"

"Doc says she's about three months in."

"Okay, so you have about what, six more to go?"

"Six or six and a half."

"Good. You have at least six months to get over this fear of what may never happen, and live your life, Bert. Her friend may have had a medical condition she didn't know about, or a complication that the doctor couldn't handle. That doesn't mean Molly will go down the same path," she said, wishing Ellie or the pastor, or someone would pop in at any moment to say hi. She could deal with drunkards and outlaws all day long, but when it came to sentiment, she was lost.

"Thanks," he mumbled, wiping his face. "You're right. I've gotten myself all worked up over something that may never happen," he added, regaining his composure.

"Exactly. Now, you're going to be a father. I believe that calls for celebration."

"No whiskey!" Bert exclaimed.

Jessie shook her head. "After what I went through with you the last time, definitely not," she laughed.

***

By the end of the day, the entire town knew that Bert and Molly were expecting a child. Jessie and Ellie attended supper at their house, where Ellie was asked to be Molly's midwife. Although she knew nothing about birthing babies, she planned to be there to help wherever she could.

On their walk home, Ellie looped her arms through Jessie's and looked up at the sky full of stars, surrounding the full moon. "It's a beautiful night," she murmured.

"It is," Jessie replied, looking at her instead of the sky. "I wish it was cold...maybe even snowing, right now."

"Why is that?"

"So we could lie naked together on a blanket in front of the stove." She smiled.

"I was thinking more along the lines of trying to squeeze into the bathing tub together to cool off in this heat," Ellie said.

"Now, that…is a good idea, Mrs. Henry," Jessie uttered, as they walked into the General Trade.

"Aren't you working tonight?" Ellie asked as Jessie followed her up the stairs to their living quarters. The brightness from the moon shined through the window, casting the space they called home, in a soft glow.

"I told Elmer to send for me if something goes awry," she said, removing her hat. "I figured Bert and Molly needed a night to let everything sink in…. besides, I wanted to spend some time with my wife. Is that okay?" she added, loosening her gun belt. "If you want me to go work—"

"I want you right here," Ellie whispered, reaching for the buttons on her vest.

Jessie leaned forward, meeting her lips in a sensual kiss, before helping her remove the layers of clothing between them, one piece at a time. By the time they were naked, they were already on the bed, trading touches.

"What happened to the bath?" Jessie asked between kisses.

Ellie rolled on top of her. "Do you really want to stop now?"

Jessie shifted her leg between Ellie's legs and grinned at the wetness that coated her thigh. She pulled Ellie down into another searing kiss that left them both breathless.

***

Boone Creek

Dark clouds hung low in the sky in the distance, potentially threatening Boone Creek with a thunderstorm. They'd had a few storms already, but nothing like a major summer storm, full of lightning and heavy rain. The rancher and farmers on the outskirts of town welcomed the heavy rains which helped grow their crops, but in town, the storms just caused a nasty mess.

"That doesn't look good," Jessie said, leaning against the post outside of the doorway to Marshal's Office. She had her eyes on the looming clouds.

"Maybe it'll stay away," Bert mumbled.

Jessie saw Ellie standing outside of her store, doing the same thing. She briefly thought about the night before as they lie together, panting and sweating with the moonlight illuminating the room. She smiled and tilted her head, listening further when she thought she'd heard thunder. Then, she saw a handful of men on horses race past, ripping through town.

"What's going on?" Bert asked.

"I don't know." Jessie watched as they turned down Center street.

***

"Claire! I know you're here!" one of the men yelled, riding his horse down the middle of the Six Gun Alley.

"There's no Claire here," said one of the town folk who was walking by.

The man on the horse, leading the charge, pulled his gun and shot the friendly bystander in the arm. He fell to the ground, bleeding. The man did nothing as he dismounted his horse and tore through the Rustler's Den, then Miss Mable's, shouting, "Claire! Claire!"

Graysen Morgen

"Maybe she ain't here," one of the other men uttered.

"Oh, she's here," he growled, getting back on his horse. "Claire! You ought to come on out before anyone else gets hurt!" he shouted.

***

"Marshal!" a young teenager yelled, running up the sidewalk. "Come quick! An outlaw just shot a man over in Six Gun."

"Who the hell *is* that?" she mumbled.

"Someone said the McNally Gang."

"McNally?" She looked at Bert. "Jasper McNally? What in the world would he be doing all the way out here?" she said, thinking out loud.

"Do you know him?" Bert asked.

"No. I know of him, though. They're nothing but thieves and murderers," she replied, wondering what he would be doing in their town as she stepped outside and looked down the street. "Who the fuck is Claire?" she questioned, hearing his ranting.

"I have no idea," Bert answered with a shrug.

"Stay here," she said, running across the way, just before the gang moved back to Main Street, with the lead guy staying on his horse, while the others went in and out of each building. "Stay inside and lock the door," she said to Ellie as she went inside the store.

"You're not going after them." Ellie shook her head. "Jessie, no."

"I have to, Ellie. They've already shot one person."

"You can't stop him," she said. "He's here for me."

"What? What do you mean?"

193

"That man out there yelling is Jasper McNally, and he's very dangerous," Ellie muttered.

Jessie raised her brows in surprise. "How do you know this?" she asked.

"Because I murdered his little brother, Wilbur McNally. My first name is really Claire."

Jessie gasped in shock. "What? When was this?"

"I married Will when I was sixteen. A year later, I was pregnant with our child…that was the first time he hit me. I lost the baby not long after that. He hit me some more because it was my fault that I lost it." She shook her head, dredging up old memories that she'd buried deep down. "After two more years of him hitting me, almost daily, I'd had enough."

"What did you do?" Jessie questioned.

"I scrapped together loose coins whenever I could, hiding them under a floorboard in the house. He had an old pistol that he said didn't shoot straight. He laughed one day and gave it to me in case someone came up when he wasn't there, saying I'd be dead anyway. Well, it just so happens that that pistol did shoot straight. I waited for him to wander in drunk one night, ready to slap me around good. I stood in front of the door and as he walked in, I shot him right between the eyes." She glanced at Jessie, who had a stunned look on her face, and sighed, "He's here because he wants revenge."

"You were just a kid," Jessie said, shaking her head in disbelief.

"I murdered him in cold blood."

"You were being beaten. That's self defense."

"It doesn't matter in his eyes, or the justice for that matter. I had no right to kill him," she said softly. "It took him five years to finally find me."

"How did you wind up here?" Jessie asked, still trying to wrap her head around what she was hearing. "We lived about a half days ride from Dodge City in a place called Rosewood Pass, in a one room adobe. The gang was spread out around the pass in the surrounding adobe huts. Will told me when they'd first arrived, there was a small Indian settlement there. The gang cleared out the Indians and made it their home. My family is in Dodge City. That's where I met Will. He promised a life full of riches and happiness, so I ran off with him and got married. I had no idea he was an outlaw, until it was too late. Anyway, when I shot him, I took his horse and rode into Dodge City. From there, I sold a few furs and some silver pots. That got me a train ticket out west. I went to Tombstone for a bit, where I worked in a restaurant. That's where I met Cornelius Fray, not long after. He was kind and gentle. We were soon married and moved here two years ago to start a life together. We opened the store, and six months later, Corny was killed, right out front, as you know." She paused. "I despise gangs. They've taken so much from me. I'm pretty sure Will's beatings are the reason Corny and I never had a child." She wiped away a stray tear. "Outlaws are nothing but woman beaters, thieves, and murderers. They should all be shot dead," she spat, brushing away a few more tears. "I should've never stopped running. I knew Jasper would find me one day."

"You're done running," Jessie said, heading for the door.

"Jessie, no! Please, don't go out there," she begged, but it was too late, she'd already stepped out into the street.

Jessie stepped off the sidewalk, just as Jasper was coming up on the theatre and the General Trade, with his gang.

"Do I know you?" he said, staring up and down at the person in front of him.

"You're not welcome here," she said. "You've already broken several laws as it is."

"A woman...wait a minute..." he stammered at the law officer being female, then was taken aback as recognition set in. "Well, well, well, look at what we got here, boys, if it isn't Jessie 'La Diabla' Henry...wearing a badge, no less," he laughed. "I heard you were dead," he added shaking his head.

"Wait until the Eldorado Gang finds out their fearless leader traded them for a badge!"

"I already told you, I don't want any trouble," she said calmly.

"Are you serious?" he laughed again, looking at his brother, Cecil. "Tell me they didn't make one of the deadliest outlaws in the south, a town marshal!"

Jessie moved her hand to her pistol, knowing she was outnumbered. There was no way she could draw on him, but she wasn't sure she had a choice. "You're right. I am the Town Marshal, and I've already told you, we don't want any trouble."

"This town is harboring someone who belongs to me. Stay out of this, La Diabla. I have no beef with you."

"You just created beef with me by coming into my town, causing a ruckus. I hear you shot a man, too."

Jasper ignored her and pulled his pistol, shooting it into the air. "You have until dusk to come out, Claire!" he shouted. "Or I'll go door to door and drag you out by your pretty, long hair!"

"And if she doesn't?" Jessie said.

"I'll burn this town to the ground," he yelled, kicking his horse to make it run as he fired his gun in the air. His two brothers rode in a circle, shooting their guns in the air, before following him out of town.

"What the hell was all that?" Bert asked, running over to her.

Jessie ignored him as she turned back towards the store and went in search of Ellie.

"You're an outlaw?" Ellie cried, pushing her away when Jessie tried to hold her. "Is it true? What is La Diabla?"

"Ellie?" Jessie sighed.

"Answer me!" Ellie growled.

"She-devil or female devil," Jessie muttered.

"So, it's true?"

"Yes," Jessie stated. "I led a gang. I did a lot of bad things. I won't deny it, but Ellie, I've changed my ways. I turned my life around."

"How could you lie to me?" Ellie cried.

"I never meant to hurt you," Jessie said, taking a step towards her.

"Get away from me!" Ellie screamed.

Jessie hung her head and walked out of the store.

TWENTY-FOUR

Several town folk had heard the exchange between the marshal and the outlaw, and it didn't take long for word to begin to spread like wildfire.

"What was that all about? Is it true?" Bert asked as Jessie walked into the Marshal's Office.

She had no time to answer as the mayor rode up on his horse. "We need to talk," he said, tying it to the post after he'd climbed down. "Bert, you can wait outside."

"Look me in the eye and tell me you haven't made a fool of me," he growled.

"Have I ever crossed you? Have I ever disobeyed the laws here? No," she asked and answered herself. "I have a past. I won't deny it. It made me who and what I am today."

"I'm in shock," he mumbled. "I mean…I knew you weren't exactly a law abiding citizen when you came to town, but knowing you're a gang-leading outlaw…I feel like I've been deceived. Hell, the whole town does." He shook his head.

"If you want my badge, ask for it. But I'm telling you this…I'm going to stop the McNally brothers."

"I don't even know why they're here, and who the hell is this Claire they're looking for?"

"It's Ellie, but that's her story to tell. I only just found out myself. I'm not going to let them hurt her, or anyone else, whether it's still my job or not, doesn't matter."

"I guess you both have secrets," he said.

"Mayor, everyone has a past. Some are just much deeper than others," she replied, knowing that stopping the gang and keeping them from destroying the town or hurting anyone else, was the only way she could prove her worth. She pushed the door open and walked out into the street. Several business owners and town folk were out on the sidewalks, gossiping and looking her way.

"I was once Jessie 'La Diabla' Henry, leader of the Eldorado Gang," she said loudly. "I made a lot of bad decisions, and did some horrible acts, but that's not who I am anymore. I am Boone Creek Town Marshal, Jessie Henry, now. Those of you who have to come to know me, know I am not dangerous. But those men who were just here, they're more than dangerous…and they're coming back. This is my home, my town, and I'm not going to let any gang, no matter who it is, come into Boone Creek and threaten the good people who live here. I took an oath to uphold the law and keep the peace here, and that's what I plan to do. Anyone who wishes to join me, can find me in the saloon."

***

A few patrons were scattered around the Rustler's Den when Jessie walked in, taking a seat at the bar. "Whiskey," she said, nodding to Elmer.

"For the record, I don't care," he muttered, sliding the glass over to her. "I'd rather have an ex-outlaw running the law of the town than some two-bit sissy."

"Thanks," she sighed, taking a long swallow of the burning liquor.

"I knew there was something about you the day you walked in here like it was nothing, after having just shot a man to death. Don't get me wrong, he deserved it," Elmer said. "I don't think it was your intention to become the marshal and mislead everyone."

"No." Jessie shook her head. "I came here to leave my old life behind, but a job was asked of me, a job I knew I could do. At first, I looked at it as a penance for a life of crime, but this town…the people…everything grew on me. I'd finally found a place that felt like home." She handed him the empty glass and sighed, "Otis was right, the mayor should've never made me the town marshal."

"You're wrong. That old drunk is full of shit. Making you the town marshal was the best decision Mayor Montgomery has ever made. He probably won't admit, but I guarantee you he'd do it all over again tomorrow if he had to. You've done a fine job as our town marshal, and you've made some friends along the way, and fell in love. There's certainly nothing wrong with any of that."

"Yeah, well the whole town hates me."

"I don't," Bert said, walking into the saloon. "You had your reasons for not telling anyone about your past. Do I think you should've been upfront about it, yes, but there's nothing you can do about that now. The town is being threatened and you're the only one who can stop it. You're the town marshal. I stand with you as your deputy…and your friend."

"We are with you, too, Marshal Henry," another man said. He had two more men behind him.

Jessie hadn't seen any of them enter the saloon after Bert. She stared for a second, unsure of what to stay, as no words were coming to her.

"See," Elmer mumbled. "You've made an impression on this town, outlaw or not, they're ready to stand behind you."

Jessie nodded and took a long look at each of the men. "The McNally brothers gang is out for blood. I can't guarantee you won't get hurt, or worse," she stated.

"I don't care, as long as it helps save this town from those vicious bastards!" one man yelled.

"I'm with him," another said.

"We're here to help you, Marshal. Whatever you need us to do, you just say it," the first guy added.

Jessie looked at Bert, shaking her head in surprise. "I guess we'd better find the mayor so he can deputize them," she said, rounding up the small group and leading them out of the saloon.

***

Mayor Montgomery was out in the street, not far from the saloon, dealing with a handful of complaining town folk. Some were calling for his resignation for appointing an outlaw as the town marshal. Others, including Otis, wanted her relieved of duty as the town marshal, and thrown out of town.

"Lock her up!" Otis yelled as he stumbled around. "I knew she was bad news. I tried to tell you."

"Oh, give it a rest, Otis!" the mayor said. "In fact, all of you, just shut up for a minute." He turned to Jessie and the men. "What's going on?"

201

"I need you to temporarily deputize these men. They've offered to join me in going after the McNally brothers," she replied.

"I don't think that's a wise idea," he said.

"It's not over. They're coming back tonight, and they'll keep coming back until they get what they want."

"They're obviously after you. You probably crossed them," Otis uttered.

"No." Jessie shook her head. "I'm not who they're looking for, but I'm prepared to give my life trying to stop them from getting it." She looked at Mayor Montgomery. "Let me finish this...my way. Then, if you want, I'll resign and leave Boone Creek...for good."

"All right, but you're not taking any of our town folk with you. I won't allow you to put them in harm's way."

"We're not asking for your permission," one of the men said.

"Nope. I don't need to be no deputy to help save my town," another stated.

Jessie rested her hands on her gun belt and pinned the mayor with a stare.

"Fine," he huffed. "You gentlemen are all willing to put your lives on the line for an outlaw who is going after another outlaw?"

"No, we're standing behind our town marshal when she needs help defending the place we all call home!" the third man exclaimed.

"I don't have badges for you, but Bert can be your witness, just the same," the mayor said. "Hold up your right hands and repeat after me," he continued, deputizing the three men to assist with law matters pertaining to the McNally brothers gang only. "This temporary authorization will expire in twenty-four hours time," he finished.

"We won't need twenty-four hours," Jessie uttered. "Let's meet in the Marshal's Office in twenty minutes," she said to the group, before walking away with Bert at her side. "I want you to stay behind, when we go."

"Me? What for? I'm a trained law officer. These guys—"

"Are not about to become a father. At least, not that I know of." She looked at him. "I could never face Molly, or your child, if something happened to you. Besides, when this is all over, you're probably going to become the town marshal, so there's no need to go out there and get yourself killed."

"You're the town marshal now, and you will be when this is over...because I'm going with you. This is my home, too. This is where my kid will grow up. I'd rather be a father who kept his oath as a deputy and helped stopped a gang, than one who stood by and did nothing."

"Even if I order you to stay back?" she asked.

"I won't disobey an order."

"Good," she replied, opening the door of the Marshal's Office.

Bert removed his badge from his vest and handed it to her. "I don't have to follow your orders if I'm no longer a law officer."

"Damn it, Bert!" She shook her head and gave his badge back to him. "I'm not going to talk you out of this, am I?"

"No."

Jessie crossed her arms. "You need to go talk with Molly. She may not even be aware of what's going on."

"She is. As a matter of fact, she's with Ellie."

Just the sound of her name made Jessie's heart ache. "Fine. We have work to do." She pulled a map of the town from her desk drawer. "If he's threatening to come back at dusk, he can't be far away," she said, studying the terrain. "I'm thinking Pinewood Pass is our best option. The McNally brothers are more than likely out there in the valley with the vagrants. That's the closest habitable area, unless they're in the mining camp, but I doubt that."

"I agree. Pinewood and Red Rock are too far away," he said, looking at the area.

"We'll sneak down the pass and wait at the base of Boone Mountain, using the tree line as cover. As soon as they come out of the valley and enter the pass, we'll cut them off."

"Sounds like a plan."

"When the new deputies arrive, bring them up to speed and meet me at the stables. I'm going to go get us some horses."

***

The town's people who knew what was going on, stood around the street and sidewalks, patiently awaiting…for what, they weren't sure. All they knew was their town marshal led a small posse of men, including her deputy, out of town. Since they'd gone towards Pinewood Pass and left from the stable, which was nearby, most of the town folk had no idea they'd even gone, until the news began to spread.

TWENTY-FIVE

Armed with sawed-off, double-barrel shotguns, known as stage guns, the three interim deputies waited nervously near the horses inside the tree line. Bert and Jessie had moved closer to the edge to get a better view. Wait until they come up on us," Jessie said, "And keep those horses quiet. Bert, you take the right flank, and I'll take the left. We'll go out in front of them, guns aimed high. If they draw, we shoot. Understand?"

Everyone mumbled the word yes, as they each kept their eyes peeled.

"It shouldn't be long now. We're about a half hour from dusk," she added, spinning the wheel clip of her revolver, making sure it was fully loaded.

"I see something," Bert whispered, looking through the monocular tube. "It's...a horse. Wait, there are three of them."

"Do you see the McNally brothers?"

"Yes. Sorry, they're up on the horses, and heading this way."

Jessie watched the group ride closer and closer. "Here we go," she whispered.

"I know you're out there somewhere, La Diabla," Jasper called out. "Give me Claire, or I'll kill everyone in that town, starting with you!"

"You're under arrest by the Town of Boone Creek!" she yelled.

Jasper laughed and fired his pistol into the air.

"Now!" Jessie shouted, rushing out of the trees on foot with her pistol aimed at the men.

Jasper pointed his gun at her and Jessie pulled the trigger, hitting him square in the chest. He flipped backwards off his horse as blood began pouring from the bullet hole in the center of his tan shirt, just above the brown vest he was wearing.

Bert ran out of the trees just after Jessie shot Jasper. The two brothers opened fire on the wooded area at the same time. Jessie dove for Bert, knocking him to the ground as she pulled the trigger, hitting one of the brothers in the side of his head. The temporary deputies returned fire from their position, killing the third brother and his horse.

Bert got up from the ground and looked back at the woman who had dove in front of him, saving his life, as she limped towards Jasper's body.

The other deputies cheered as they rushed out of the woods and rounded up the two McNally brother's horses.

"You and your brothers will never hurt her again," Jessie whispered, spitting on the ground next to Jasper's head. She tried to focus as she walked towards her horse, but the pain in her side was nearly unbearable. She reached down, winching as she pushed her palm against her side. It was tinged with warm blood when she pulled it away. "We need to bring them back...with us," she mumbled.

Bert helped the other deputies drape the McNally brothers' bodies over the back of three horses. He noticed Jessie stumble and slip, nearly doubling over each time she tried to mount her mare. Rushing to her side, he said, "Let me see it."

"I'm...fine."

"You're shot!" he cried, seeing the blood when he pulled her hand away.

"How bad is it?" one of the men asked, rushing over to help.

"We have to get her back, now!" Bert yelled.

"Bert...calm down. I can ride," she said through clenched teeth.

"You can't even get on a horse, Marshal," the other deputy replied.

"Help me get up. I can...do it."

Bert and one of the deputies lifted her into the saddle as she growled in pain, still holding her side.

"You three go ahead. I'll stay back with her," Bert said to the extra men.

"We're doing this together," one man replied as they mounted their horses.

With Jessie leading, the group trotted back up the pass, towards Boone Creek.

***

The thirty-minute ride back to town seemed to take forever. Jessie struggled to focus on the trail and control the reins with one hand, while squeezing with her legs as hard as she could to keep herself upright.

When they entered the town limit, they headed past the mayor's office, towards the Marshal's Office around the curve. Jessie brought her horse to a stop. The men slowed behind her, quickly tying the horse's reins to a hitching post.

Several of the town folk were milling about, awaiting their return after a few men had reported hearing gunfire out near the valley. People gasped at the sight of the dead men, draped over the back of the horses.

"Someone get Doc Vernon, now!" Bert shouted.

Hearing his voice, Molly went outside to see what all the commotion was, and Ellie followed her. The mayor had seen them ride by from his office window, and rushed down the street.

Bert and one of the deputized men helped Jessie from her horse, while the other men tossed the gang members' bodies on the ground. She nearly crumbled to the ground, but they caught her and held her up.

"Anyone who has a problem with this courageous, respectable woman being our Town Marshal, has a problem with me," Bert yelled to the people lining the sidewalk in front of the businesses and standing in the street to get a closer look.

"Us too," the deputized men said. "These men won't be a threat to this town anymore. She just about single-handedly took them out herself!" they added, pulling the men's bodies from the horses and laying them out on the ground.

"If it wasn't for her...I'd be lying here with them," Bert added somberly. "She saved my life."

"Clear the way!" Doc Vernon yelled, coming through the crowd. "Oh my!" he gasped, seeing the dead men, one with only half a head.

"It's not them. It's her!" one of the deputies exclaimed, pointing to Jessie, who's eyes were half lidded.

Doc Vernon pulled Jessie's blood-soaked hand from her side.

"Bring her in here!" Ellie yelled, clearing a path to her store.

Bert and the other deputy helping to keep Jessie on her feet, each grabbed one of her legs and placed their other arms behind her back.

"Wait!" Mayor Montgomery blurted. "Jessie Henry, you're hereby decreed the Town Marshal of Boone Creek, Colorado Territory until you perish or otherwise resign because you're too damn old to do it anymore. You hear me?" he said, smiling slightly as he placed his hand on her shoulder. "Now, go on, Doc! Get her fixed up! We don't need our marshal dying on us, do we folks?" he said, putting his hands up and turning around, as if awaiting their answer.

Everyone in the street began to cheer and clap.

Bert and the deputy carried Jessie inside and laid her on the floor on her back. The temporary deputy joined the other two, placing their backs to the doctor and his patient, while forming a barricade to conceal what was happening behind them. Molly hurried down the stairs with a bowl full of water and towels for the doctor's use.

Ellie dropped to the floor on her knees next to Jessie's good side. "I'm so sorry," she whispered through tears.

"You're safe...now," Jessie whispered.

"I love you. Please don't leave me," Ellie cried, brushing a hand along her soft cheek. "I couldn't bare losing you. You have my whole heart, Jessie. You and only you," she sobbed as wet tears flowed down her cheeks, soaking the sleeve of Jessie's white shirt.

"Drink this," Doc Vernon said, handing her a small bottle of opium from his bag. He picked her head up so that she could swallow. "Now," he continued, putting her head back on the ground. "Bite down on this." He shoved a leather satchel strap into her mouth. It stuck out on both sides as she clenched down.

Ellie unbuttoned Jessie's vest and helped the doc lift her bloody shirt up high enough for him to reach her side. A nasty hole, about the size of a finger tip, was located near the bottom of her rib cage. Blood continued to ooze out of it as he palpated the area.

Jessie lurched and cried out when he touched her.

"This is going to hurt like hell," he said, shoving the forceps inside the hole.

Jessie screamed as she bit the strap between her teeth.

"Hold her still!" the doc yelled.

Bert knelt down beside him and put his hands on Jessie's hip to keep her steady, with Ellie practically sitting on her opposite side, while the doctor searched around for the bullet in her side.

"Here we are," Doc Vernon stated, pulling the fragment out. "It bounced around her ribs, so a few of them are probably fractured, but it didn't go any deeper." He stuck his finger in the hole as Jessie screamed and writhed under the two people holding her down. "There's some definite tissue damage, but nothing too serious," he added, removing his finger and wiping away the blood. "All done," he said, smiling at Jessie as he patted her shoulder with his clean hand. "I'm going to stitch you up now."

"She's going to be okay?" Ellie asked.

"Oh...yeah. She'll be in pain for a while, but it'll heal."

"Thank God," Ellie murmured. She looked back, feeling a hand on her shoulder. Pastor Noah stood back behind her, holding his bible. He nodded and smiled at her.

"I told you...you'd...never...lose me," Jessie mumbled as the effects of the opium began to kick in. "I...love you...Ellie," she slurred, before passing out.

Ellie smiled and bent down, kissing her sweaty cheek. "I love you, too," she whispered, "Forever."

About the Author

Graysen Morgen is the bestselling author of *Falling Snow*, *Fast Pitch*, *Cypress Lake, Meant to Be, Coming Home*, the Never Series: *Never Let Go* and *Never Quit*, the Bridal Series: *Bridesmaid of Honor*, *Brides*, and *Mommies*, as well as many other titles. She was born and raised in North Florida with winding rivers and waterways at her back door, as well as, the white sandy beach. She has spent most of her lifetime in the sun and on the water. She enjoys reading, writing, fishing, coaching and watching soccer, and spending as much time as possible with her wife and their daughter.

You can contact Graysen at graysenmorgen@aol.com; like her fan page on Facebook.com/graysenmorgen; follow her on Twitter: @graysenmorgen and Instagram: @graysenmorgen

Other Titles Available From
Triplicity Publishing

Witness by Joan L. Anderson. Becca and Kate have lived together for eight years, and have always spent their vacation in a tropical paradise, lying on a beach. This year, Becca wanted to try something different: a seven day, 65-mile hike in the beautiful Cascade Mountains of Washington state. Their peaceful vacation turns to horror when they stumble upon a brutal murder taking place in the back country.

Too Soon by S.L. Gape. Brooke is a twenty-nine year old detective from Oxford, who has her life pretty much planned out until her boss and partner of nine years, Maria, tells her their relationship is over. When Brooke finds out the truth, that Maria cheated on her with their best friend Paula, she decides to get her life back on track by getting away for six weeks in Anglesey, North Wales. Chloe, a thirty three year old artist and art director, owns a log cabin on Anglesey where she spends each weekend painting and surfing. After returning from a surf, she stumbles upon the somewhat uptight and enigmatic Brooke.

Blue Ice Landing by KA Moll. Coy is a beautiful blonde with a southern accent and a successful practice as a physician assistant. She has a comfortable home, good friends, and a loving family. She's also a widow, carrying a burden of responsibility for her wife's untimely death. Coby is a woman with secrets. She's estranged from her family, a recovering alcoholic, and alone because she's convinced that she's unlovable. When she loses her job as a heavy equipment operator, she'll accept one that'll force her to step way outside her comfort zone. When Coy quits her job to accept a position in Antarctica, her path will cross with Coby's. Their attraction to one another will be immediate, and despite their differences, it won't be long before they fall in love. But for these two, with all their baggage, will love be enough?

Never Quit (Never Series book2) by Graysen Morgen. Two years after stepping away from the action as a Coast Guard Rescue Swimmer to become an instructor, Finley finds herself in charge of the most difficult class of cadets she's ever faced, while also juggling the taxing demands of having a home life with her partner Nicole, and their fifteen year old daughter. Jordy Ross gave up everything, dropping out of college, and leaving her family behind, to join the Coast Guard and become a rescue swimmer cadet. The extreme training tests her fitness level, pushing her mentally and physically further than she's ever been in her life, but it's the aggressive competition between her and another female cadet that proves to be the most challenging.

For a Moment's Indiscretion by KA Moll. With ten years of marriage under their belt, Zane and Jaina are coasting. The little things they used to do for one another have fallen by the wayside. They've gotten busy with life. They've forgotten to nurture their love and relationship. Even soul mates can stumble on hard times and have marital difficulties. Enter Amelia, a new faculty member in Jaina's building. She's new in town, young, and very pretty. When an argument with Zane causes Jaina to storm out angry, she reaches out to Amelia. Of course, she seizes the opportunity. And for a moment of indiscretion, Jaina could lose everything.

Never Let Go (Never Series book 1) by Graysen Morgen. For Coast Guard Rescue Swimmer, Finley Morris, life is good. She loves her job, is well respected by her peers, and has been given an opportunity to take her career to the next level. The only thing missing is the love of her life, who walked out, taking their daughter with her, seven years earlier. When Finley gets a call from her ex, saying their teenage daughter is coming to spend the summer with her, she's floored. While spending more time with her daughter, whom she doesn't get to see often, and learning to be a full-time parent, Finley quickly realizes she has not, and will never, let go of what is important.

Pursuit by Joan L. Anderson. Claire is a workaholic attorney who flies to Paris to lick her wounds after being dumped by her girlfriend of seventeen years. On the plane she chats with the young woman sitting next to her, and when they land the woman is inexplicably detained in Customs. Claire is surprised when she later runs into the woman in the city. They agree to meet for breakfast the next morning, but when the woman doesn't show up Claire goes to her hotel and makes a horrifying discovery. She soon finds herself ensnared in a web of intrigue and international terrorism, becoming the target of a high stakes game of cat and mouse through the streets of Paris.

Wrecked by Sydney Canyon. To most people, the *Duchess* is a myth formed by old pirates tales, but to Reid Cavanaugh, a Caribbean island bum and one of the best divers and treasure hunters in the world, it's a real, seventeenth century pirate ship—the holy grail of underwater treasure hunting. Reid uses the same cunning tactics she always has before setting out to find the lost ship. However, she is forced to bring her business partner's daughter along as collateral this time because he doesn't trust her. Neither woman is thrilled, but being cooped up on a small dive boat for days, forces them to get know each other quickly.

Arson by Austen Thorne. Madison Drake is a detective for the Stetson Beach Police Department. The last thing she wants to do is show a new detective the ropes, especially when a fire investigation becomes arson to cover up a murder.

Madison butts heads with Tara, her trainee, deals with sarcasm from Nic, her ex-girlfriend who is a patrol officer, and finds calm in the chaos of police work with Jamie, her best friend who is the county medical examiner. Arson is the first of many in a series of novella episodes surrounding the fictional Stetson Beach Police Department and Detective Madison Drake.

Change of Heart by KA Moll. Courtney Holloman is a woman at the top of her game. She's successful, wealthy, and a highly sought after Washington lobbyist. She has money, her job, booze, and nothing else. In quiet moments, against her will, her mind drifts back to her days in high school and to all that she gave up. Jack Camdon is a complex woman, and yet not at all. She is also a woman who has never moved beyond the sudden and unexplained departure of her high school sweetheart, her lover, and her soul mate. When circumstances bring Courtney back to town two decades later, their paths will cross. Will it be too late?

Mommies (Bridal Series book 3) by Graysen Morgen. Britton and her wife Daphne have been married for a year and a half and are happy with their life, until Britton's mother hounds her to find out why her sister Bridget hasn't decided to have children yet. This prompts Daphne to bring up the big subject of having kids of their own with Britton. Britton hadn't really thought much about having kids, but her love for Daphne makes her see life and their future together in a whole new way when they decide to become mommies.

Haunting Love by K.A. Moll. Anna Crestwood was raised in the strict beliefs of a religious sect nestled in the foothills of the Smoky Mountains. She's a lesbian with a ton of baggage—fearful, guilty, and alone. Very few things would compel her to leave the familiar. The job offer of a lifetime is one of them. Gabe Garst is a police officer. She's also a powerful medium. Her work with juvenile delinquents and ghosts is all that keeps her going. Inside she's dead, certain that her capacity to love is buried six feet under. Anna and Gabe's paths cross. Their attraction is immediate, but they hold back until all hope seems lost.

Rapture & Rogue by Sydney Canyon. Taren Rauley is happy and in a good relationship, until the one person she thought she'd never see again comes back into her life. She struggles to keep the past from colliding with the present as old feelings she thought were dead and gone, begin to haunt her. In college, Gianna Revisi was a mastermind, ring-leading, crime boss. Now, she has a great life and spends her time running Rapture and Rogue, the two establishments she built from the ground up. The last person she ever expects to see walk into one of them, is the girl who walked out on her, breaking her heart five years ago.

Second Chance by Sydney Canyon. After an attack on her convoy, Marine Corps Staff Sergeant, Darien Hollister, must learn to live without her sight. When an experimental procedure allows her to see again, Darien is torn, knowing someone had to die in order for this to happen.

She embarks on a journey to personally thank the donor's family, but is too stunned to tell them the truth. Mixed emotions stir inside of her as she slowly gets to the know the people that feel like so much more than strangers to her. When the truth finally comes out, Darien walks away, taking the second chance that she's been given to go back to the only life she's ever known, but she's not the only one with a second chance at life.

Meant to Be by Graysen Morgen. Brandt is about to walk down the aisle with her girlfriend, when an unexpected chain of events turns her world upside down, causing her to question the last three years of her life. A chance encounter sparks a mix of rage and excitement that she has never felt before. Summer is living life and following her dreams, all the while, harboring a huge secret that could ruin her career. She believes that some things are better kept in the dark, until she has her third run-in with a woman she had hoped to never see again, and gives into temptation. Brandt and Summer start believing everything happens for a reason as they learn the true meaning of meant to be.

Coming Home by Graysen Morgen. After tragedy derails TJ Abernathy's life, she packs up her three year old son and heads back to Pennsylvania to live with her grandmother on the family farm. TJ picks back up where she left off eight years earlier, tending to the fruit and nut tree orchard, while learning her grandmother's secret trade. Soon, TJ's high school sweetheart and the same girl who broke her heart, comes back into her life, threatening to steal it away once again. As the weeks turn into months and tragedy strikes again, TJ realizes coming home was the best thing she could've ever done.

Special Assignment by Austen Thorne. Secret Service Agent Parker Meeks has her hands full when she gets her new assignment, protecting a Congressman's teenage daughter, who has had threats made on her life and been whisked away to a Christian boarding school under an alias to finish out her senior year. Parker is fine with the assignment, until she finds out she has to go undercover as a Canon Priest. The last thing Parker expects to find is a beautiful, art history teacher, who is intrigued by her in more ways than one.

Miracle at Christmas by Sydney Canyon. A Modern Twist on the Classic Scrooge Story. Dylan is a power-hungry lawyer who pushed away everything good in her life to become the best defense attorney in the, often winning the worst cases and keeping anyone with enough money out of

jail. She's visited on Christmas Eve by her deceased law
partner, who threatens her with a life in hell like his own, if
she doesn't change her path. During the course of the night,
she is taken on a journey through her past, present, and future
with three very different spirits.

Bella Vita by Sydney Canyon. Brady is the First Officer
of the crew on the Bella Vita, a luxury charter yacht in the
Caribbean. She enjoys the laidback island lifestyle, and is
accustomed to high profile guests, but when a U.S. Senator
charters the yacht as a gift to his beautiful twin daughters who
have just graduated from college and a few of their friends, she
literally has her hands full.

Brides (Bridal Series book 2) by Graysen Morgen.
Britton Prescott is dating the love of her life, Daphne Attwood,
after a few tumultuous events that happened to unravel at her
sister's wedding reception, seven months earlier. She's happy
with the way things are, but immense pressure from her family
and friends to take the next step, nearly sends her back to the
single life. The idea of a long engagement and simple wedding
are thrown out the window, as both families take over, rushing
Britton and Daphne to the altar in a matter of weeks.

Cypress Lake by Graysen Morgen. The small town of
Cypress Lake is rocked when one murder after another
happens. Dani Ricketts, the Chief Deputy for the Cypress Lake
Sheriff's Office, realizes the murders are linked. She's
surprised when the girl that broke her heart in high school has
not only returned home, but she's also Dani's only suspect.
Kristen Malone has come back to Cypress Lake to put the past
behind her so that she can move on with her life. Seeing Dani
Ricketts again throws her off-guard, nearly derailing her plans
to finally rid herself and her family of Cypress Lake.

Crashing Waves by Graysen Morgen. After a tragic accident, Pro Surfer, Rory Eden, spends her days hiding in the surf and snowboard manufacturing company that she built from the ground up, while living her life as a shell of the person that she once was. Rory's world is turned upside when a young surfer pursues her, asking for the one thing she can't do. Adler Troy and Dr. Cason Macauley from Graysen Morgen's bestselling novel: *Falling Snow*, make an appearance in this romantic adventure about life, love, and letting go.

Bridesmaid of Honor (Bridal Series book 1) by Graysen Morgen. Britton Prescott's best friend is getting married and she's the maid of honor. As if that isn't enough to deal with, Britton's sister announces she's getting married in the same month and her maid of honor is her best friend Daphne, the same woman who has tormented Britton for years. Britton has to suck it up and play nice, instead of scratching her eyes out, because she and Daphne are in both weddings. Everyone is counting on them to behave like adults.

Falling Snow by Graysen Morgen. Dr. Cason Macauley, a high-speed trauma surgeon from Denver meets Adler Troy, a professional snowboarder and sparks fly. The last thing Cason wants is a relationship and Adler doesn't realize what's right in front of her until it's gone, but will it be too late?

Fate vs. Destiny by Graysen Morgen. Logan Greer devotes her life to investigating plane crashes for the National Transportation Safety Board. Brooke McCabe is an investigator with the Federal Aviation Association who literally flies by the seat of her pants. When Logan gets tangled in head games with both women will she choose fate or destiny?

Just Me by Graysen Morgen. Wild child Ian Wiley has to grow up and take the reins of the hundred year old family business when tragedy strikes. Cassidy Harland is a little surprised that she came within an inch of picking up a gorgeous stranger in a bar and is shocked to find out that stranger is the new head of her company.

Love Loss Revenge by Graysen Morgen. Rian Casey is an FBI Agent working the biggest case of her career and madly in love with her girlfriend. Her world is turned upside when tragedy strikes. Heartbroken, she tries to rebuild her life. When she discovers the truth behind what really happened that awful night she decides justice isn't good enough, and vows revenge on everyone involved.

Natural Instinct by Graysen Morgen. Chandler Scott is a Marine Biologist who keeps her private life private. Corey Joslen is intrigued by Chandler from the moment she meets her. Chandler is forced to finally open her life up to Corey. It backfires in Corey's face and sends her running. Will either woman learn to trust her natural instinct?

Secluded Heart by Graysen Morgen. Chase Leery is an overworked cardiac surgeon with a group of best friends that have an opinion and a reason for everything. When she meets a new artist named Remy Sheridan at her best friend's art gallery she is captivated by the reclusive woman. When Chase finds out why Remy is so sheltered will she put her career on the line to help her or is it too difficult to love someone with a secluded heart?

In Love, at War by Graysen Morgen. Charley Hayes is in the Army Air Force and stationed at Ford Island in Pearl Harbor. She is the commanding officer of her own female-only service squadron and doing the one thing she loves most, repairing airplanes. Life is good for Charley, until the day she finds herself falling in love while fighting for her life as her country is thrown haphazardly into World War II. Can she survive being in love and at war?

Fast Pitch by Graysen Morgen. Graham Cahill is a senior in college and the catcher and captain of the softball team. Despite being an all-star pitcher, Bailey Michaels is young and arrogant. Graham and Bailey are forced to get to know each other off the field in order to learn to work together on the field. Will the extra time pay off or will it drive a nail through the team?

Submerged by Graysen Morgen. Assistant District Attorney Layne Carmichael had no idea that the sexy woman she took home from a local bar for a one night stand would turn out to be someone she would be prosecuting months later. Scooter is a Naval Officer on a submarine who changes women like she changes uniforms. When she is accused of a heinous crime she is shocked to see her latest conquest sitting across from her as the prosecuting attorney.

Vow of Solitude by Austen Thorne. Detective Jordan Denali is in a fight for her life against the ghosts from her past and a Serial Killer taunting her with his every move. She lives a life of solitude and plans to keep it that way. When Callie Marceau, a curious Medical Examiner, decides she wants in on the biggest case of her career, as well as, Jordan's life, Jordan is powerless to stop her.

Igniting Temptation by Sydney Canyon. Mackenzie Trotter is the Head of Pediatrics at the local hospital. Her life takes a rather unexpected turn when she meets a flirtatious, beautiful fire fighter. Both women soon discover it doesn't take much to ignite temptation.

One Night by Sydney Canyon. While on a business trip, Caylen Jarrett spends an amazing night with a beautiful stripper. Months later, she is shocked and confused when that same woman re-enters her life. The fact that this stranger could destroy her career doesn't bother her. C.J. is more terrified of the feelings this woman stirs in her. Could she have fallen in love in one night and not even known it?

Fine by Sydney Canyon. Collin Anderson hides behind a façade, pretending everything is fine. Her workaholic wife and best friend are both oblivious as she goes on an emotional journey, battling a potentially hereditary disease that her mother has been diagnosed with. The only person who knows what is really going on, is Collin's doctor. The same doctor, who is an acquaintance that she's always been attracted to, and who has a partner of her own.

Shadow's Eyes by Sydney Canyon. Tyler McCain is the owner of a large ranch that breeds and sells different types of horses. She isn't exactly thrilled when a Hollywood movie producer shows up wanting to film his latest movie on her property. Reegan Delsol is an up and coming actress who has everything going for her when she lands the lead role in a new film, but there one small problem that could blow the entire picture.

Light Reading: A Collection of Novellas by Sydney Canyon. Four of Sydney Canyon's novellas together in one book, including the bestsellers Shadow's Eyes and One Night.

Visit us at www.tri-pub.com

Made in the USA
Lexington, KY
21 June 2017